KT-151-849

fairy
secrets

Gwyneth Rees is half Welsh and half English and grew up in Scotland. She went to Glasgow University and qualified as a doctor in 1990. She is a child and adolescent psychiatrist, but has now stopped practising so that she can write full-time. She is the author of the bestselling Fairies series (*Fairy Dust, Fairy Treasure, Fairy Dreams, Fairy Gold, Fairy Rescue*), *Mermaid Magic, Cosmo and the Magic Sneeze* and *Cosmo and the Great Witch Escape*, as well as several books for older readers. She lives in London with her family.

Visit www.gwynethrees.com

C153299100 WITHDRAWN

Books by Gwyneth Rees

Mermaid Magic
Fairy Dust
Fairy Treasure
Fairy Dreams
Fairy Gold
Fairy Rescue
Cosmo and the Magic Sneeze
Cosmo and the Great Witch Escape

The Magical Book of Fairy Fun
Cosmo's Book of Spooky Fun

For older readers

The Mum Hunt
The Mum Detective
The Mum Mystery
The Mum Surprise (World Book Day 2006)
The Making of May
My Mum's from Planet Pluto

And coming soon
Cosmo and the Secret Spell

fairy secrets

Fairyland could be lost forever!

Gwyneth Rees

Illustrated by Emily Bannister

MACMILLAN CHILDREN'S BOOKS

First published 2008 by Macmillan Children's Books
a division of Macmillan Publishers Limited
20 New Wharf Road, London N1 9RR
Basingstoke and Oxford
Associated companies throughout the world
www.panmacmillan.com

ISBN 978-0-330-44215-2

Text copyright © Gwyneth Rees 2008
Illustrations copyright © Emily Bannister 2008

The right of Gwyneth Rees and Emily Bannister to be identified as
the author and illustrator of this work has been asserted by them in
accordance with the Copyright, Designs and Patents Act 1988.

All rights reserved. No part of this publication may be
reproduced, stored in or introduced into a retrieval system, or
transmitted, in any form or by any means (electronic, mechanical,
photocopying, recording or otherwise), without the prior written
permission of the publisher. Any person who does any unauthorized
act in relation to this publication may be liable to criminal
prosecution and civil claims for damages.

1 3 5 7 9 8 6 4 2

A CIP catalogue record for this book is available from
the British Library.

Typeset by Tony Fleetwood
Printed and bound in the UK by CPI Mackays, Chatham ME5 8TD

This book is sold subject to the condition that it shall not,
by way of trade or otherwise, be lent, resold, hired out,
or otherwise circulated without the publisher's prior consent
in any form of binding or cover other than that in which
it is published and without a similar condition including this
condition being imposed on the subsequent purchaser.

This book is for Ellen Tullett,
who is half Welsh like me

KENT LIBRARIES & ARCHIVES	
C153299100	

'This is going to be the most boring holiday ever,' Ellie's older brother, David, complained as their train came to a halt at the station where they had to get off.

But Ellie wasn't listening. She had already spotted their aunt, who had promised to meet them at the railway station with her car. It had taken several hours on the train to get this far, and now Ellie couldn't wait to get outside.

'Hi, Aunt Megan!' she called out excited-ly as she stepped down on to the platform. Aunt Megan was their dad's older sister, who lived in a small village in south Wales. She wasn't married and didn't have any children, and she had always doted on David and Ellie.

Aunt Megan looked the same as ever, with her slightly old-fashioned hairstyle and her sensible but colourful clothes, and Ellie

ran to her straight away to give her a hug.

'Don't bother helping with the bags or anything, will you?' David grumbled from behind her.

'Oh, David, what a big boy you're getting!' Aunt Megan exclaimed – which was what she always said when she saw him and which never failed to make him cringe. 'It must be at least two years since you were here,' she added as she helped him with the cases.

'It's three,' Ellie corrected her. 'I was six and David was eleven. Though we only stayed for the weekend then.'

'Is it really that long since you were here? You're getting so grown-up, travelling all this way on your own.'

'It wasn't that difficult,' Ellie pointed out. 'Mum and Dad put us on the train and all we had to do was sit in our seats.'

3

'Yeah – though they were fussing so much, they obviously reckoned we wouldn't even be able to do *that* without getting into trouble,' David added drily. 'Not that Ellie would dare get out of her seat, in any case. She'd be far too scared in case somebody spoke to her.'

Ellie scowled at him. OK, so she knew she was shy, but it didn't help to have him make fun of her because of it.

'The car's just over here,' Aunt Megan said as they walked into the station car park. 'It's a bit of a drive, as you know.'

Aunt Megan lived on the edge of a village in a beautiful valley, and Ellie had been looking forward to coming to stay ever since their aunt had invited them. It was the first weekend of the summer holidays, and their mum and dad were flying abroad tomorrow and would be gone for a whole week. David had wanted to stay at home alone, but he hadn't been allowed to.

David climbed into the front of the car and Ellie got in the back. At first Ellie tried to join in the conversation from the back seat, but it was very hot in the car and she soon nodded off.

She didn't realize how long she had slept until she woke to find that they'd stopped at a small petrol station. It had 'Owen's Garage' written on a big sign outside – along with something in Welsh that Ellie didn't understand. Ellie remembered the garage from their visit three years earlier. It was on the main road that led into Aunt Megan's village. She was about to point out to David that they were nearly at their destination when she noticed he had fallen asleep too.

Aunt Megan was standing beside the car, chatting to the old man who was filling up their petrol tank. (This was the only garage Ellie had ever been to that wasn't self-service, though she remembered her aunt saying that all petrol stations had had pump-attendants in the old days.) Ellie reckoned the old man must be Mr Owen, the owner.

She yawned and was about to wind down her window to get some fresh air when she thought she saw something moving inside the garage shop. She stared for a bit longer, and yes – there were definitely two yellow things flitting about on the counter. Curious, she opened her door and climbed out to go and take a closer look.

'Are you all right, Ellie?' Aunt Megan asked.

She nodded, stepping quickly past her aunt and heading for the open door of the shop. There was an old-fashioned till on the counter and something yellow and fluttery immediately disappeared behind it. She hurried over and peered behind the till.

'Wow!' she cried out, because there, hovering in the air, supporting a bar of chocolate between them, were two fairies in yellow petal dresses.

Ellie was speechless with shock. Although she had always *believed* in fairies, this was the first time she had ever actually seen one.

The fairies were clearly shocked too, because they shrieked when they saw her, and dropped the chocolate bar on the floor. In a matter of seconds they had whizzed out of the open door and vanished.

'Wait!' Ellie called out, running outside after them.

Before she even had time to pinch herself to see if she was dreaming, Mr Owen came to join her. 'Saw some of our fairies, did you?' he asked.

Normally the fact that a stranger was talking to her would have made her blush, but now she was too amazed by what she had just seen to worry about anything else.

'We're pretty well populated with them in this valley,' he added.

'But ... but ... Aunt Megan never ...' She trailed off. Her aunt had never mentioned that there were fairies living in the valley, and Ellie certainly hadn't seen any the last time she'd been here.

'Oh, your auntie doesn't believe in them. That's why she never gets to see any. Fairies are only visible to people who believe in them – like you and me. The fairies always come to *my* shop for their chocolate supplies because they know I'll realize it was them and won't go blaming anyone else when a bar or two goes missing.'

'The fairies steal chocolate from your shop?' Ellie could hardly believe it.

'Oh, they don't steal it. They exchange it. They always leave me something in return.' He walked past her to the confectionary stand. 'It's here with the chocolate bars, see – a fairy flower bracelet!'

Ellie gasped in delight as he lifted up a sparkly bracelet made of lots of fresh flowers threaded together, large enough to fit on a small human wrist.

'It's the fairy dust that makes it sparkle like that,' the old man explained. 'Those flowers won't wilt for months. Here. You can have it if you like.'

'Thank you!' she exclaimed, hardly able to contain her excitement as she slipped it on to her wrist and found that it was exactly the right size.

'Shame they left their chocolate bar behind,' he said, bending down to pick it up. 'It's broken so I won't be able to sell it now. You may as well have that too.'

Ellie could hear her aunt calling to her. 'I'd better go,' she said quickly.

As he handed her the broken chocolate he said, 'The fairies will definitely come and see you tonight if you leave this out on your window ledge for them.' He chuckled. 'They're greedy little things really. Some of them have got quite fat tummies, if you get close enough to have a look!'

"ELLIE – HURRY UP!" David's voice reached her now, much less patient than her aunt's. He had obviously woken up and was in a grouchy mood.

As soon as she got back into the car Ellie showed her aunt and brother the bracelet and told them about seeing the two fairies.

David started laughing. 'You're crazy!'

'No, I'm not! Mr Owen says there are lots of fairies here!'

'Well, he's crazy too then! Everyone knows there's no such thing!'

'If there's no such thing as fairies then

☆ ☆ ☆ 11

who do you think made *this*?' Ellie demanded, thrusting the fairy bracelet under his nose. 'The fairies left it for Mr Owen and he gave it to me.'

David looked at it scornfully. 'It's just some silly flower bracelet that some little kid probably left in his shop.'

'No, it's not!' she protested. 'It's a *fairy* bracelet, David. Can't you see how sparkly it is?'

Clearly David couldn't – and neither could Aunt Megan, although she wasn't as rude about it as David.

'Mr Owen has been telling everyone about the fairies for as long as I can remember,' their aunt said in a trying-to-keep-the-peace sort of voice, as she started up the car. 'A lot of folk in the village believe in them.'

'Great,' David muttered sarcastically. 'So

we've come to spend a whole week in a village full of nutters. You should fit right in, Ellie.'

'David – that's not very nice, is it?' Aunt Megan scolded him.

'He's *never* nice,' Ellie said, glaring at her brother. 'Anyway, I don't care what he thinks. I'm going to leave this chocolate bar on my window ledge tonight, because Mr Owen says that's the way to get the fairies to come and visit me.'

'Oh, well. If you're just going to do *that* with it . . .' And before she could stop him, David had reached back and snatched the chocolate from her hand.

'Give that back!' she screeched, but he was already ripping off the wrapper to take a bite.

Aunt Megan was too busy manoeuvring the car out on to the main road to stop him,

13

though she did sound cross as she said, 'Oh, David, that's very unkind!'

But David, who had already shoved the whole thing into his mouth, just laughed.

Aunt Megan sighed. 'Tell you what, Ellie,' she said, looking at her niece sympathetically in the rear view-mirror. 'I've made a lovely chocolate cake for tea this afternoon and I've decorated it with chocolate buttons. Why don't you leave some of *those* out for your fairies instead?'

'OK,' Ellie said, though she still felt furious with David. If their parents were there, he'd never have dared act like that.

'You're such a baby, thinking fairies are real, Ellie,' David jibed, his mouth still stuffed full of chocolate.

'I don't just *think* it – I *know* it!' Ellie retorted. 'I told you. I just saw two of them in Mr Owen's shop!'

14

'Yeah – right!' David snorted.

Then Aunt Megan said something surprising. 'Don't you remember the time *you* saw a fairy, David? You were about four, I think. You and your parents were staying with me and you came running into the house, very excited. You said you'd found a fairy in my fishpond, and you wouldn't stop talking about her for hours!'

'I don't remember that,' David said, sounding irritated.

'Well, *I* do.' Aunt Megan started to laugh. 'You kept saying you had rescued her from being eaten by a fish!'

'See?' Ellie said gleefully. 'So don't you dare make fun of *me* for believing in fairies!'

'Well, I was only four then, wasn't I?' David retorted. 'I was too young to know any better. You're *nine*, in case you've forgotten!'

They were still arguing about whether or not fairies were real when they arrived at Aunt Megan's cottage a few minutes later.

'Come on, you two! That's enough,' Aunt Megan said, ushering them into the house. 'Let's have some tea. I've been baking all week for you coming.

2

When it was time for bed that night, Ellie left all the chocolate buttons she had saved from her piece of cake on the window ledge, just as Mr Owen had suggested. Unfortunately she was sharing Aunt Megan's spare bedroom with David, so she made sure she picked the bed nearest to the window, and that she left the curtains open so she could keep an eye on the chocolate buttons after she'd put them on the ledge. Then she lay down facing the window to wait.

She needn't have worried about David,

because he was so tired after their long journey that he fell asleep almost as soon as he'd got into bed. Before she knew it, however, she felt her own eyes starting to close too. She tried her hardest to stay awake, but soon she was so fast asleep that she didn't hear the flutter of wings and the whispering of tiny voices as two fairies landed on the windowsill.

After exclaiming in delight at the chocolate buttons, one of the fairies flew right inside the children's room. She had bright green eyes, short, light brown curly hair and a very cheeky freckled face. Her dress was made from two layers of daffodil petals and she wore a pink cardigan made from finely spun local sheep's wool. She flew straight over Ellie and stopped when she reached David.

She peered down at him excitedly. 'It's

him, Bronwen!' she called out. 'He's a lot bigger but it's definitely the same boy. I knew I recognized him at the garage.'

The second fairy had flown into the room now. She had brown eyes, dark hair that fell sleek and straight to just below her shoulders and she wore an altogether more solemn and sensible expression. Her dress was also made of daffodil petals and her woollen cardigan was a pale lilac colour with pretty buttons made from sparkly birdseeds.

'Myfanwy, isn't that the little girl who made us drop our chocolate?' she said, glancing at Ellie, who was still fast asleep.

'Yes, she must be his sister or something. Oh, wasn't it kind of him to leave us all those chocolate buttons? I *told* you he was kind! And brave! His name's David – and if it wasn't for him, goodness knows what would have happened to me when I fell into that pond!' She had flown even closer to his face now. 'See how handsome he's become. Oooh – I wish he would wake up! Do you think if I poked him a little bit . . . ?'

'No, Myfanwy!' Bronwen warned, but the fairy was already prodding at David's nose with a tiny finger.

'If only I'd brought my wand with me,' Myfanwy said impatiently. 'The jagged edges would be sure to wake him.'

'Leave him alone, Myfanwy! You know Queen Lily says we're not allowed to wake children when they're sleeping, unless it's an emergency!'

'Well, Queen Lily won't find out, will she? Not unless someone tells her.' Myfanwy grinned cheekily at Bronwen, whom she knew was far too good a friend to do that.

Just then Ellie started to stir in her bed.

'The little girl's eyelids are flickering – that means she's about to wake up,' Bronwen warned. (Every fairy was very good at spotting when a human was about to wake.) 'Come on, Myfanwy! Let's go!'

The two fairies flew back out on to the windowledge and started to collect up the chocolate buttons, placing them one on top of the other to make two small stacks.

'This one's got a bit of cake icing stuck to it – yummy!' Myfanwy said, licking her lips.

'Hurry up, Myfanwy!' Bronwen urged her. Through the open window she could see Ellie opening her eyes and sitting up in bed, and by the time Ellie was fully awake, each fairy was balancing a little stack of chocolate buttons on her head as she took off from the windowsill.

'Wait!' Ellie cried out, jumping out of bed and running to the window.

But by
the time she
got there,
the fairies were
already halfway across the garden,
and they didn't look back.

The next morning was Sunday and when
Ellie told Aunt Megan about the fairies her
aunt smiled and said, 'What a wonderful
imagination you've got!' Before Ellie could
protest that it wasn't just her imagination
Aunt Megan announced that she was taking
them to visit the toy museum in the village

that afternoon. 'I'm sure you'll find it very interesting. My friend Mr Daniels owns it and though it's usually closed on Sundays he says he'll open it today, just for us. It's only a small museum but it's got lots of different antique toys and—'

'I'm too old to be interested in toys,' David interrupted scornfully.

'Very well, I'll just take Ellie then,' Aunt Megan said swiftly. 'We'll go this afternoon.' She shot David a sly glance as she added, 'And we'll have a nice cream tea while we're out, Ellie, since the museum is so close to the village tea shop.'

Ellie grinned and looked at her brother, who she knew loved cream teas just as much as she did.

'I suppose I *could* come for the tea,' David grunted, sounding like he was offering to do them a huge favour.

Aunt Megan nodded. 'All right then, David – but only if you're sure. I wouldn't want you forcing yourself to eat a cream tea on my account! Ellie and I will go to the museum and we'll meet you in the tea shop afterwards.'

So that afternoon Ellie and her aunt set off for the toy museum, which turned out to be a large stone house with a grey slate roof, situated in the centre of the village. It had wooden stairs on the outside, leading up to a white door at the top, and both the staircase and the door looked like they badly needed a new coat of paint. Above the door was a hand-painted sign saying 'Toy Museum' twice – once in English and once in Welsh.

'Mr Daniels's father started the museum fifty years ago, and when he died it passed on to Daniel. He lives in the downstairs

part of the building,' Aunt Megan told her as she led Ellie up the stairs to the door, which was propped open.

'Is Mr Daniels's *first* name *Daniel* as well then?' Ellie asked in surprise.

'It certainly is,' a friendly Welsh voice answered, and she turned to see a smiling old man with a bald head and large dark eyes standing in the doorway. 'Daniel Daniels at your service,' he said, shaking her hand. 'It *is* a bit of a mouthful, isn't it?'

Ellie blushed and the old man laughed.

'Daniel, this is my niece, Ellie,' Aunt Megan said, smiling.

'Very pleased to meet you, Ellie,' the old man said cheerily. 'Like old things, do you?'

'Well …' Ellie hadn't really thought about whether she liked old things or not and in any case, she was feeling too embarrassed by the attention he was giving her to be able to think straight.

'Well, why don't you have a look round and see what you think?' he said. 'I'm guessing a lot of these old toys aren't all that different from the ones you young ones have today.'

So Ellie went into the large room that housed the museum while her aunt followed Mr Daniels into his office to have a chat.

'Any news?' Ellie heard her aunt ask.

'Not good, I'm afraid,' Mr Daniels replied.

Ellie couldn't hear their conversation after that, and in any case her attention had been caught by the museum room, which had glass cases fixed all around the walls, containing lots of old toys. In the cabinet nearest to her Ellie saw an old wooden train set, a sailing boat, a tin monkey, some musical instruments, a couple of thick wooden jigsaws (one of which was still in its original box), some wooden farm animals, a pile of old comics and a jack-in-the-box. The next cabinet held wooden skittles, several skipping ropes, a spinning top, an ancient-looking dolls' pram and a child's tricycle as well as an assortment of hoops and balls. A large wooden dolls' house sat in the next cabinet on its own, and in the centre of the room another glass case housed all the old dolls and teddies. Right at the front of that cabinet, seated around a little square picnic rug (which had a doll-sized teapot and four teacups laid out on it), were four toys that Ellie found herself particularly drawn to.

Sitting on one side of the rug was a very old yellow teddy bear, whose amber-coloured glass eyes seemed to be looking straight at Ellie. He had several bald patches

in his fur, and his mouth had disintegrated at the ends so that he looked quite sad.

Positioned opposite him was a plump china doll. Blonde wavy hair fell down around her pretty face, which had two dimples in the cheeks and a trace of pink still remaining on the rosebud lips. Her eyes were blue and made of glass and she had eyelids that looked like they would close if you laid her down. She wore a frilly blue dress (which had been hitched up on one side to show off her long frilly knickers) and she had only one shoe, made of the same blue material as her dress.

On the right of the china doll was a Welsh costume doll, with a soft body and very fine features painted on to her stockinet face. She had brown eyes with perfect little dark lashes, a sweet little red mouth and a delicate nose. Her black hair was arranged in two neat plaits, and she wore a red velvet dress with a blue checked apron and matching shawl. Her hat was a traditional tall black Welsh one, made of felt, with a trimming of white lace under the brim.

The last of the four toys that had been placed around the rug was a painted wooden soldier who wore a red uniform with gold buttons. His paint was faded now rather than shiny, but he must have once looked very smart indeed. He had a little wooden rifle (painted silver) attached to his hand, and black marching boots on his feet.

The toys looked to Ellie as if they might be in the middle of a silent conversation with each other and she couldn't stop staring at them.

Suddenly she saw something yellow moving inside the glass case. Could it be another fairy? Excited, she hurried round to the opposite side of the case to see if she could spot it there, but whatever it was, it had vanished as quickly as it had appeared.

'Ellie, have you finished?' Aunt Megan called out to her from the doorway. 'Mr Daniels needs cheering up so he's going to come with us for our cream tea.'

Reluctantly Ellie left the cabinet and went to join her aunt. But as she glanced back she was sure she saw the china doll's skirt moving slightly as if something was hiding beneath it.

'Aunt Megan, why does Mr Daniels need cheering up?' Ellie whispered, as they walked with him along the narrow pavement towards the village tea shop.

'Really, Ellie, you *can* speak to Mr Daniels directly,' Aunt Megan told her. 'I know speaking to people you don't know makes you nervous, but it sounds very rude if you talk about them as if they're not here when they're standing right beside you!'

'Sorry,' Ellie mumbled, flushing bright red.

'Oh, there's nothing wrong with being a bit shy,' Mr Daniels put in quickly. 'I was shy when I was a lad – though you'd never know it now!' He smiled kindly at her. 'Ellie, the reason your aunt reckons I need cheering up is because I'm going to have to sell my museum soon.'

'Really? What's going to happen to all the toys then?' Ellie couldn't help wondering if they might need new homes, in which case . . .

'Unfortunately all the toys have to be included in the sale,' Mr Daniels told her, shaking his head as if he didn't agree with that. 'A businessman from London wants to buy the whole building and knock it down so that he can rebuild on the land. But he has a daughter who's about your age and he wants to give the toys to her.'

'*All* the toys?' Ellie was amazed. 'She won't have room for *all* of them, will she?'

'This man is very wealthy and apparently his daughter is an only child and she has a whole floor of the house to herself.'

'She sounds rather spoilt to me,' Aunt Megan said, clicking her tongue. 'A whole floor of the house indeed!'

Ellie didn't say anything but she couldn't help wishing that she could change places with this girl, just for a little while, to see what it would be like to have all that space to yourself, with no big brother to annoy you.

'I dare say I should count myself lucky really,' Mr Daniels continued. 'This fellow was here on holiday and noticed my advert asking for donations to keep the museum going. He came to see the building and offered to buy it from me. Normally I'd never have agreed, but I just can't afford to keep the place going as it is, and at least this way I won't be in debt any more. I'll even have enough money left over to buy myself a little cottage to live in.'

'But I really like your museum,' Ellie said, frowning.

'So do I,' Mr Daniels replied, and Ellie noticed a tear in his eye. 'It breaks my heart to let it go, it really does. But what choice do I have?'

Aunt Megan put her arm through his.

'I'm so sorry, Daniel,' she said. 'I just wish there was something I could do . . .'

'It's all right, my dear,' Mr Daniels said, patting her hand. 'Don't you worry about me. It's not the end of the world, and I'm sure I'll feel a lot better after a nice cream tea, eh, Ellie?'

He smiled then, clearly trying to be brave, but Ellie knew that underneath he was still sad, and that a cream tea wasn't really going to make any difference. If only there was something *she* could do to help save the museum. But right at that moment she couldn't think what.

Ellie was still thinking about the toy museum when she went to bed that night – so much so that she forgot to leave any chocolate out on her windowsill for the fairies. So when she was woken in the night by a noise in her room, she didn't guess at first that the fairies had come back.

Then she spotted them. In the dim light she could just make out two fluttering creatures hovering above her brother's bed, holding the glass of water she always kept on her bedside table at night. As she watched, they tipped up the glass and let some of the water spill out on to her sleeping brother's face.

He woke with a start and yelled out crossly, immediately reaching for the bedside lamp. The fairies quickly dodged out of the way, and when the light came on Ellie couldn't see them any more.

David was glaring furiously at her. 'What do you think you're doing?'

'It wasn't me – it was the fairies!' she defended herself. 'They just splashed some water on you!'

'Yeah – *right*!' he retorted.

Just then one of the fairies came flying out from her hiding place on the other side of David's bed. 'I'm sorry, David, but we needed to wake you up,' she told him, hovering directly in front of his face and clasping her hands together excitedly as she spoke. 'I'm Myfanwy – you do still remember me, don't you?'

As Ellie stared open-mouthed at the fairy, who she now recognized as being one of the two she had previously seen at Mr Owen's garage, David continued to glare at his sister, and it was clear that he was totally unaware of Myfanwy's presence. 'Ellie, if you don't shut up with all this fairy rubbish I'm going to . . .' He paused, sensing something wasn't quite right. 'What is it? What are you staring at?'

'Can't you see her?' Ellie whispered.

'See *who*?'

'Oh no!' Myfanwy exclaimed, clearly upset, as David got out of bed and headed for the bathroom, muttering that he was going to dry his face on a towel.

As soon as he was out of earshot Ellie finally found the courage to speak to the fairy. 'David doesn't believe in fairies any

more. That's why he can't see you,' she told
her in an apologetic voice.

Myfanwy turned to stare at her. She
looked horrified.

'Are . . . are you the fairy he rescued when
he was little?' Ellie continued shyly.

'Yes,' Myfanwy answered, sounding as if
she still couldn't believe that her hero had
deserted her. 'I was playing hide and seek
with a dragonfly and I accidently fell into
your aunt's fishpond. My wing got caught
in some weeds and I was stuck under the
water. I was ever so frightened because a
big goldfish looked like it wanted to take a
bite out of me! But then David reached in
with his fishing net and scooped me out.
After he'd rescued me I asked him to take
me to the bottom of the garden, where I
knew the other fairies would find me. Such
a caring little boy he was . . . which is why

I knew . . . at least I *thought* I knew . . . that he'd be able to help us now.'

'Help you with what?' Ellie asked curiously.

Just then the second fairy flew out to join her friend. 'Myfanwy thought David might know of a way to save the toy museum,' she explained. 'I'm Bronwen, by the way.'

Ellie smiled at her before saying, 'I *went* to the toy museum today. Mr Daniels is very upset about having to sell it, isn't he?'

'He isn't the only one,' Bronwen said gloomily. 'It's a disaster for the toys too. The poor things are horrified.'

'*Can* toys be horrified?' Ellie asked in surprise.

'Of course they can!' Myfanwy said. 'And *we're* frightened too. If the museum closes we won't be able to come to this valley any more, because the toy museum is *also* our entrance to Fairyland.'

Before Ellie could react, Bronwen snapped crossly, 'Be *quiet*, Myfanwy! You *know* that's meant to be a secret!' She looked apologetically at Ellie and added, 'I'm sorry but there are certain fairy secrets that we're not supposed to tell any human – not unless we have special permission from our fairy queen.'

'Don't worry – I would *never* give away a fairy secret,' Ellie burst out excitedly. 'But this is amazing! Does Mr Daniels know that the entrance to Fairyland is in his museum?'

'*He* doesn't even believe in fairies!' Myfanwy exclaimed scornfully. '*He's* no use to us at all, which is why we came here to ask David to help us. Our fairy queen already gave us permission to tell *him* about it.'

'I can try and help you instead, if you like,' Ellie offered.

'We'll go and tell Queen Lily about you right now and ask her if that's all right,' Bronwen said. 'She's up in the hills looking after a sheep with an injured leg, and we've to go and help her as soon as we're finished here. I expect we'll be busy for most of the night, but tomorrow we'll send you a message and let you know what she says.'

'What sort of message?' Ellie asked, but at that point David came back into the room – and within seconds both fairies had flown away.

The following morning, as Ellie was still wondering what sort of message the fairies could possibly send her, a sheep with a bandage round one of its legs appeared in Aunt Megan's back garden. The garden backed on to fields, and Aunt Megan assumed that the sheep must have come through a gap in her fence, though when she searched she couldn't find one.

'It's a mystery how she got inside,' Aunt Megan said. 'We'd better shoo her up the drive, along the road to the nearest gate and back into her field that way, I suppose.'

But every time they tried to approach the sheep it ran away in the wrong direction. Finally Ellie crept up to it on her own, and to everyone's surprise the ewe stayed put. When she got close enough Ellie saw that the animal's bandage had sparkly dust on it, and that's when she realized that the sheep must be the same one the fairy queen had been helping the previous night. Then she noticed, tucked into its bandage, a tiny sparkly envelope.

Ellie quickly grabbed the envelope and

slipped it into her skirt pocket before her aunt or David had time to see. Then she led the sheep – who went with her obediently now – out of Aunt Megan's garden and along the country road until they reached the nearest farm gate.

'You're a regular little shepherdess, Ellie,' Aunt Megan complimented her as she followed a short way behind, and Ellie could tell that even her brother was impressed.

Once the sheep was safely back in its field Ellie waited for her aunt and brother to turn back towards the house before opening the fairy letter. Inside the envelope was a folded sheet of sparkly paper, which had tiny flowers pressed around the edges and sparkly fairy writing. It said:

COME TO THE TOY MUSEUM AT 3 O'CLOCK THIS AFTERNOON. THE DOOR WILL BE OPEN.

To her amazement, each word vanished as she read it, and by the time she had read the whole message, both the paper and its envelope had completely disintegrated into a shower of golden dust.

That afternoon Ellie told her aunt she was going into the village to buy a postcard to send to her parents. Her aunt nodded her consent without hesitation, but David looked suspicious and said, 'Why do you want to send them a postcard when *they're* on holiday too?'

'I just want to. OK?' she said, scowling at him.

Ellie reached the museum at ten minutes to three and, since her aunt had already told her that Mr Daniels had gone to see his solicitor that afternoon, she hurried up the outside staircase and tried the door handle, half expecting it to be locked. But she discovered to her relief that it was open, just as the fairies had said it would be.

Quickly she slipped inside and closed the door behind her. She was now standing in the small entrance hall, with the door that led to the museum on her right, and the door to Mr Daniels's office straight in front of her. She had expected Myfanwy and Bronwen, and possibly even some other fairies, to be there, so she wasn't surprised when she heard the sound of muffled voices coming from the museum room. Nervously she tiptoed over to the closed door and knocked.

There was silence for several moments, then an unfamiliar growly voice called out, 'Who's there?'

'It's me – Ellie.' Slowly she pushed open the door and entered the room, expecting to see the fairies.

Instead she saw the four toys she had admired on her precious visit, sitting on the floor around the picnic rug with the dolls' tea set laid out in front of them.

'Hello,' the teddy bear growled.

Ellie felt the blood drain from her face as the costume doll said something in Welsh that she didn't understand and the toy soldier said, 'I'm so sorry but I believe I'm going to sneeze. A-A-A-TCHOO!'

'Do you *have* to sneeze all over our picnic?' snapped the china doll. 'I don't suppose you've got a clean hanky, have you?' she added, swivelling her head sharply to look at Ellie.

And that's when everything became a hazy blur and Ellie felt the room slipping away from her.

4

'Bronwen, this is all your fault,' Ellie heard a familiar fairy voice say as she opened her eyes. 'If you'd let me tell her in the first place, it wouldn't have come as such a shock.'

'Yes, well, *I* didn't know you wouldn't be outside to meet her like you said you'd be, did I?' Bronwen retorted.

'I only went to get some chocolate for the tea party. How was I to know she'd be early?'

'She was only ten minutes early!'

'Bronwen ... Myfanwy ...' Ellie sat up and rubbed her head, which she must have bumped when she fell. 'What happened?'

The two fairies were hovering over her looking anxious. 'Ellie, are you all right? We didn't mean you to get such a fright. You weren't meant to see the toys until we had explained things to you.'

Everything was coming back to Ellie now. 'I don't understand,' she began. 'The toys, they were . . . they were . . .'

'*Alive?*' Myfanwy finished for her, grinning. 'That's the other secret of our toy museum, you see. The toys are always coming to life when there's nobody about to see them!'

'I don't believe it,' Ellie muttered.

'You must do,' Myfanwy said impatiently. 'Otherwise you wouldn't have seen them. Only people who *believe* in toys coming to life can actually see them do it. That's part of the magic.'

'Not *all* the toys can come to life,' Bronwen added quickly. 'The person who made the toy *and* the child who first owned it both have to have believed in fairies for it even to be possible. Quite a lot of toymakers believed in fairies in the old days, but hardly any do now. That's why it's mostly only *old* toys that come to life.'

Ellie stood up slowly. It was hot and stuffy in the museum, which was probably another reason for her faint. Luckily she hadn't really hurt herself and now she looked curiously at the four toys sitting around the picnic rug. Watching her with gleaming eyes were the teddy bear, the toy soldier and the two dolls she had seen earlier. The other toys, as far as she could see, were all still in their cabinets.

One by one, the four toys introduced themselves.

'I'm Tedi,' the teddy bear said in a much less growly voice than before. 'It's spelled the Welsh way, not the English way,' he added. His mouth was now finished off at the ends with some sparkly dust, so that he looked smiley instead of sad.

'That's T-E-D-I,' the Welsh costume doll spelled out for her. 'I'm Dilys and I'm presuming you don't speak Welsh. Is that right?'

'Yes, sorry,' Ellie admitted meekly. 'My dad's Welsh and he knows a little, but he hasn't spoken it since he was a boy.'

Dilys tutted her disapproval as she reached forward to pour out the tea.

'I'm Enid,' said the china doll, whose missing shoe had been replaced with a sparkly new one and whose knickers were no longer on display.

'And I'm Llewellyn,' announced the toy

soldier, giving her an earnest salute. His paint looked shinier than the last time she had seen him and his gold buttons and silver gun were gleaming. 'I'm sorry if my sneeze startled you just now. I do sneeze rather a lot, I'm afraid. It's very dusty in here, which is not what I'm used to. A soldier's barracks are always spick and span, you see.'

Ellie stared at the four of them in amazement. 'I just don't understand how it's possible . . .' she began in a shaky voice. 'I mean, I've always believed in *fairies* but . . .'

'It's not that strange really,' Bronwen explained. 'You see, if a toymaker believes in fairies, then a little bit of fairy magic goes into every toy they make . . .'

'And then if the first child who *owns* the toy believes in fairies too, that magic gets stronger,' Myfanwy continued.

'And if the toy then meets a fairy who sprinkles it with fairy dust, then the toy can come to life!' Bronwen added. 'But only until the fairy dust wears off again – then it goes back to being an ordinary toy.'

'Wow!' Ellie exclaimed, wondering if any of her toys at home were coming to life when she wasn't around to see them.

Myfanwy suddenly glanced up at the big museum clock and exclaimed, 'It's time for Queen Lily to arrive! Quick, everyone! Get ready!'

'Ellie – you'd better sit down and watch,' Bronwen told her gently. 'You're going to see some fairy magic now, so please don't be scared.'

As Ellie looked on, the picnic rug that the toys were seated around started to glow and, as Ellie watched, the rug seemed to glow more and more brightly until it began to radiate beams of light in all directions. And suddenly, along the central beam of light, a fairy started to emerge, getting bigger and bigger as she got closer.

'The toys form a sort of magic portal for us to travel through,' Bronwen whispered to Ellie. 'They have to be sitting around this rug inside the museum for it to work though.'

Ellie was speechless as the fairy came flying out from the light, her beautiful glittering wings spread out behind her. She was wearing a long yellow and cream layered dress made from several different types of daffodil petals, and draped around her shoulders was a cloak of pink lily petals. Her golden hair fell in waves down her back, and she had green eyes set in a beautiful heart-shaped face. Her pretty floral crown floated magically just above her head, and her sparkly petal shoes sprinkled golden dust wherever she flew. As she entered the room the scent of lilies accompanied her.

Ellie was too in awe to do anything but

stare, open-mouthed, as the fairy settled on top of the nearest glass cabinet and looked down at her.

'I am Queen Lily of the Valley,' the fairy queen announced, smiling sweetly at Ellie. 'And you must be the little girl Bronwen and Myfanwy have told me about.'

'Y-yes ... I'm ... I'm E-Ellie,' Ellie stammered, suddenly feeling more shy than she had ever felt in her life.

'You are the sister of the boy who saved Myfanwy from the fishpond, are you not?'

Ellie nodded. 'I-I'm sorry, but David doesn't believe in fairies any more.'

'So Bronwen and Myfanwy have told me. That is very sad. How old is he now?'

'Fourteen.'

Queen Lily sighed. 'I'm afraid that is a difficult age for any boy to believe in fairies. Still, we must not give up hope. Now ...'

She turned to face Bronwen and Myfanwy. 'As you know, I asked you to bring Ellie here so that we could ask for her help in saving the museum. But on reflection I think that even with Ellie's help, it is going to be very difficult indeed to stop the toy museum from being closed. In fact, I'm beginning to think that the most important thing we can do now is to find ourselves another valley to live in.' As Bronwen and Myfanwy gasped in dismay at this announcement, the fairy queen turned back to look gravely at Ellie. 'I don't know if my fairies have explained this to you, but entrances to Fairyland can only be formed in certain locations. Unfortunately the toy museum is the *only* location in this valley, which means that if the museum goes, then we will no longer be able to come here.'

'But we *can't* leave this valley!' Bronwen

burst out. 'If we go, then who will look after the sheep when lambing season comes? And who will help the ones who get lost on the mountain?'

'The farmers will still be here,' Queen Lily reminded her calmly. 'You know they always do their best for their sheep.'

'But they can't fly, so they can't always get there in time!' Bronwen argued, sounding close to tears.

'And what about Mr Owen who runs the garage?' Myfanwy said in a trembly voice. 'He's been ever so lonely since his wife died. How will he manage without us visiting him to cheer him up?'

Queen Lily sounded very sad as she answered. 'I don't know, Myfanwy. All I know is that this is the most beautiful of *all* the fairy valleys and I will be just as sorry to leave it as you are.'

'What about *us*?' called out an indignant voice, and everyone turned to look at Enid, who was standing up on her plump china legs looking distressed. 'If we are to be taken to this place called London that we have heard Mr Daniels speak of, then how will we come to life there?'

'Calm down, Enid,' Llewellyn the soldier said, though he also looked worried. 'Surely there are fairies in London who can help us come to life just as we do here?'

'Of course there are,' the fairy queen reassured them. 'It might take them a little while to find you, that's all.'

'But I *like* living here!' Enid exclaimed, sounding as if she might be about to have a tantrum.

'So do I!' Tedi growled angrily. 'I don't want to go to London!'

'We must not leave Wales, whatever

happens,' Dilys said passionately. 'We are Welsh toys, and I know we shall be terribly unhappy if we have to live anywhere else.'

The toys started to all talk at once until the fairy queen held up her hand for silence.

'If you are all so determined not to leave this valley, then it seems to me that there is only one thing to be done,' she announced. 'However difficult it appears, we must find a way of raising the money that Mr Daniels needs to keep the museum open. I know that *money* is not something we fairies know much about, but what we *do* know is that it is very important to humans. Ellie, you are a human. What do *you* think?'

Ellie flushed as she felt everyone's attention settle on her. The truth was that she had already seen Mr Daniels's

home-made posters pinned up around the village and according to her aunt they had generated very little response.

PLEASE HELP SAVE
OUR LOCAL
TOY MUSEUM
BY GIVING ANY DONATION
YOU CAN!

'The trouble is, people probably don't think the toy museum is such an important cause as some other charities,' she mumbled self-consciously.

'Are you saying that humans don't *care* about toys?' Dilys demanded, her dark eyes flashing.

'I think it's just that most people don't

know that toys can come to life,' Ellie explained quickly. 'Which is why they probably think it's better to give money to . . . I don't know . . .' She paused, thinking about the charities her parents supported. 'Say, the NSPCC – that's the National Society for the Prevention of Cruelty to Children – or the RSPCA – that's the charity that prevents cruelty to animals.'

'But what about *us*?' Myfanwy said impatiently. 'Surely a charity has been set up for the prevention of cruelty to *fairies*?'

Ellie shook her head, trying not to smile. 'I'm sorry. I think people either just don't *believe* in fairies or . . . or . . . they sort of assume that fairies can take care of themselves.'

The three fairies and four dolls all stared at her in dismay.

'Well, usually we *can*, of course,' Queen

Lily said finally. 'But there will always be times when we fairies need a little help from you humans.'

Ellie frowned, trying her hardest to think what *she* could do to help, while all the toys and fairies continued to stare at her expectantly. 'I suppose we could always target somebody who has a special *reason* to help the museum,' she suggested.

'Like who?' Bronwen and Myfanwy asked together.

'I don't know . . . someone with a special interest in old toys, maybe. Or someone who once donated a toy to the museum and wants to see the museum stay where it is.'

'I know, I know!' Enid burst out excitedly. 'What about the human *I* used to belong to?'

But before Ellie could even ask who that was, Tedi was shaking his head, Dilys was rolling her eyes and Llewellyn was looking impatient as he said, 'Not this again!'

Enid ignored them and announced proudly, '*I* used to belong to the Queen!'

'No, you didn't!' Dilys snapped.

'Yes, I did. You're just jealous because I'm a royal doll and you're not!'

'Enid, we've been through this before – you've no proof!' Tedi interjected.

'No toy can remember who their owner was before they first came to life,' Myfanwy quickly explained to Ellie. 'But even though Enid first came to life in this museum, she's been convinced she *does* remember her previous owner, ever since—'

'Let *me* tell her about it,' Enid butted in crossly. And she related to Ellie how one evening Mr Daniels had taken her downstairs to his living quarters in order to mend her dress while he watched television.

'There was a hypnotist on the programme,' Enid explained, 'and he demonstrated how you can hypnotize a human to make them remember things that happened to them when they were very young. Well, as he spoke it was as if his words were sending me into a trance, and all of a sudden the word "Queen" popped up in my head!'

'Yeah, right!' Dilys said sarcastically. 'And the Queen is really going to come here and help us the second she hears about a tiny toy museum closing!'

'Well, she might! Or her son might! He *is* the Prince of Wales, you know.'

'Never mind that for a minute, Enid,' Bronwen interrupted suddenly. 'I've got a much better idea.' She paused until she was sure the others were all listening. 'What about Mrs Lloyd-Hughes?'

'Who's she?' Ellie asked.

'She's a very rich widowed lady who lives
in the big manor house next to the church,'
Bronwen explained. 'She's got loads of
money and no family to leave it to, and she
quite often gives donations to local causes
that are to do with children. The thing
is, she might not have seen Mr Daniels's
posters because she's very old and frail and
she hardly ever leaves her house. If we could
persuade *her* to donate some of her money
to the museum ...'

'But how can we ask her?' Myfanwy
wanted to know. 'She doesn't believe in
fairies, so we can't even speak to her.'

'It doesn't have to be a *fairy* who asks her,
does it?' Bronwen replied, looking pointedly
at Ellie.

Everyone turned to gaze at Ellie then,
including the fairy queen.

'*Will* you help us, Ellie?' Queen Lily

asked in the gentlest of voices.

'W-wouldn't it be better if Mr Daniels asked her, rather than me?' Ellie mumbled nervously. The truth was that she was far too shy to go knocking on the door of a complete stranger to ask for help.

'Mr Daniels is too proud to ask anyone for money directly,' Queen Lily said, flying down from the top of her cabinet and stopping to hover in the air in front of Ellie's face. 'Please say you'll help us, Ellie,' she pleaded. 'You are our only hope.'

5

By the time Ellie got home, Aunt Megan was starting to wonder where she had got to.

'Surely it can't take that long to choose a postcard, Ellie,' she said when her niece finally appeared.

'Yeah. So where is it then?' David demanded. He was sitting at the kitchen table eating a big slice of chocolate cake.

'I . . . I wrote it and put it in the post box already,' Ellie quickly lied. 'Aunt Megan, I've been thinking about how we can help Mr Daniels and I've had an idea.'

She had been thinking all the way home

about the best way to come to the aid of
the fairies, and she had eventually decided
to try and enlist her aunt's help. After all,
Aunt Megan wanted to save the museum
too, didn't she?

'Really?' Aunt Megan sounded interested.
'What idea is that then?'

'Well, I just heard that there's a lady who's
very rich who lives in the village who often
donates money to good causes that are to
do with children,' Ellie said. 'Her name is
Mrs Lloyd-Hughes. So I thought maybe
you and I could go and ask her to help.'

Aunt Megan looked surprised. 'How did
you hear about her, Ellie? Has somebody
in the village been gossiping again?'
Fortunately she didn't wait for a reply
before she continued. 'It's true that Mrs
Lloyd-Hughes has funded a number of
local projects. She helped the Scouts when

they needed a new hall and she also paid for a music room in the village school. She tends to like everyone to know about her involvement though! The new Scout hall has been named after her, and every year the school has to give a concert with her as guest of honour. If *she* gave any money to the toy museum, I expect its name would have to be changed to the Lloyd-Hughes Museum.' She gave a short laugh. 'I wonder what Daniel would think of *that*!'

'Surely he'd rather have it called that than lose it altogether, wouldn't he?' Ellie pointed out.

Aunt Megan nodded. 'I suppose so. But you know, Ellie, he's already put a leaflet through every door in the village asking for donations – including hers.'

'Maybe she needs someone to ask her face to face,' Ellie said. 'I mean, if she's the sort of person who likes to feel important, she'd probably want to be asked directly rather than just have some leaflet shoved through her door.'

'You certainly *have* been thinking a lot about this, haven't you, Ellie?'

Ellie nodded. 'So can we go and ask her ourselves right now, before Mr Daniels sells his museum to that man in London?'

David, who had been listening to all of this with an incredulous expression, started to laugh. 'You do realize that you'll have to do *all* the talking when you get there, don't you, Aunt Megan?' he said. 'Ellie will just clam up.'

'No, I won't!' Ellie protested.

'Of course you will. What about last Halloween when Mum and Dad made me take you out trick-or-treating? *I* was the one who had to speak every time somebody opened the door and all *you* did was stand there with your mouth open. I felt like a right idiot.'

Aunt Megan was giving Ellie a searching look. 'I must say, knowing how shy you are, Ellie, I can't help wondering at your suggesting this.'

Ellie swallowed. To be honest her strategy *had* been more along the lines of getting Aunt Megan to talk to Mrs Lloyd-Hughes while *she* looked on.

'I'll tell you what though,' her aunt continued thoughtfully, 'if you *do* agree to try to explain all this *yourself* to Mrs Lloyd-Hughes, I *will* take you to see her.'

Ellie thought about how much the fairies needed her help. 'OK,' she said in a rush.

'You're sure?'

She nodded, though she was already beginning to feel nervous.

'You'll never do it!' David told her.

'I don't think that kind of reaction is very helpful, thank you,' Aunt Megan said briskly. 'Come on, Ellie, let's go now before we change our minds, shall we?'

Mrs Lloyd-Hughes's house was much bigger than all the others in the village. It was next to the church, just like the fairies had said, but it was separated from it by a high wall.

Ellie rang the bell and presently a thin grey-haired lady answered it, who turned out to be Mrs Lloyd-Hughes's housekeeper. 'Is she expecting you?' the housekeeper wanted to know, when Ellie had mumbled her introduction.

But before either Ellie or her aunt could answer a voice from inside the house called out crossly, 'If I've a visitor, then for goodness sake show them in, will you? If it wasn't for these useless legs of mine I'd get up and answer the door myself!'

The housekeeper kept a totally neutral expression on her face as she showed them into the living room and Ellie got the feeling she was used to Mrs Lloyd-Hughes being rude to her.

The living room had a high ceiling, huge windows, a cream carpet, cream curtains and two huge cream sofas.

'What a lovely room,' Aunt Megan said politely.

Mrs Lloyd-Hughes had snow-white hair and very dark eyes. She was seated in a high-backed cream armchair beside a massive fireplace.

'Like it too, do you?' she asked Ellie, who was staring around at the expensive-looking ornaments decorating the room.

'Oh, y-yes,' Ellie murmured, feeling herself

flushing. She knew she ought to say more but her mouth had gone completely dry.

Thankfully Aunt Megan spoke up. 'Mrs Lloyd-Hughes, I don't know if you remember me, but I think we've met a few times in church. I'm Megan Jones and this is my niece, Ellie.'

'You seem a little familiar, though it's a while since I've been to church. Tell me, what do you think of our new vicar?'

'*New* vicar?' Aunt Megan sounded surprised.

'Oh, well, he must have been here ten years or so now, but he's still an incomer as far as I'm concerned. He's from *North* Wales, you know, though he tends to keep that quiet.'

'He ... err ... seems very pleasant to me...' Aunt Megan began, but the old lady didn't seem to be listening.

'The one before him – now *he* was a lovely fellow,' she went on, 'but the one before *him* was my favourite. He married my husband and me. A very cheery young man he was – made a change from the one before *him*, who was a terrible old misery-guts. They said it was because he'd lost his wife so young – she was in her twenties when she died, poor thing. I was only a child and I remember having to get a new black dress for the funeral. That vicar only ever preached doom and gloom in his sermons after that.' She sighed. 'Oh yes, when you're eighty years old and you've lived in the same village all your life, you've seen a lot of vicars come and go.'

Ellie let out a yawn without meaning to and the old lady looked directly at her. 'Bored with the subject of vicars are you, Ellie?'

Ellie flushed bright red and couldn't speak.

'So tell me,' the old lady continued, 'why have you come to see me?'

'Well . . .' Ellie felt her face burning as she stammered, 'it's j-just that I heard you often give to charity and there's a person . . . I mean . . . well, a building . . . that's going to have to close down unless someone helps it.'

'I see. And what building is this?'

'It's the old toy museum,' Ellie replied, starting to feel a little more confident. 'It's been in this village for fifty years, but now Mr Daniels doesn't have enough money to keep it going, so he's going to have to sell it and all the toys are going to be taken away to London. He's asked for donations but he's hardly had any. I was wondering if you could help us since . . . since you've got lots of money and nobody to leave it to when you—'

'*Ellie!*' Aunt Megan interrupted, sounding mortified, but Mrs Lloyd-Hughes didn't look the least bit upset.

'Very well put, Ellie,' she said. 'I do like people to be direct rather than shilly-shallying around when they're asking me for money!'

'Mrs Lloyd-Hughes, obviously you're under no obligation—' Aunt Megan began, bright red herself now, but the old lady hushed her impatiently.

'Of course I'm under no obligation, but Ellie's right. I do have a lot of money and I don't have any relatives to leave it to when I die. However . . .' the old lady frowned, 'I'm afraid, Ellie, that I have no wish to give to this particular charity. You see, toys have made me nothing but unhappy. In fact, I hate the things!'

'But *why*?' Ellie burst out, dismayed.

'Ellie, don't be nosy,' Aunt Megan admonished her.

But Mrs Lloyd-Hughes seemed only too happy to answer. 'Because the only toy *I* ever cared about was taken away from me when I was a child, that's why!'

'But who took it?' Ellie asked, wide-eyed.

'Ellie!' Aunt Megan interrupted again.

Mrs Lloyd-Hughes suddenly looked across at her and said, 'My dear, would you be so kind as to go and ask my housekeeper to make us some tea?'

'Oh, we couldn't possibly put you to all that trouble—'

'It's my housekeeper who'll be making it and that's what I pay her for. In fact, why don't you go and have a chat with her in the kitchen while I have a chat with Ellie? After all, I don't suppose *you're* burning to know the answer to Ellie's question, are you?'

Aunt Megan looked like she didn't know how to respond, but in the end she just nodded politely and left the room. Strangely, Ellie didn't feel nearly as nervous as she normally would if she was left alone with an adult she hardly knew.

'Tell me, Ellie, do *you* have a favourite

toy?' Mrs Lloyd-Hughes asked her as soon as Aunt Megan had gone.

Ellie nodded. 'A rag doll called Trixie. She's been my favourite since I was little.'

'I see. And how would you feel if this Trixie was suddenly given away, without anyone even asking your permission?'

'I'd feel terrible!'

'Exactly. And that's how I felt when my precious china doll, Henrietta, was given away by my mother! She had been asked to donate some things to some charitable cause or other and she said she thought I was too old to be playing with dolls any more. But Henrietta was so much more than just a doll to me, Ellie. Can you understand that?' The old lady paused. 'My parents were very strict and not easy to talk to, and I had two older brothers who teased me all the time. They both died in the war, poor things, and I missed them then, but still . . . I was quite lonely as a child, what with my two brothers never letting me play with them, so I used to tell Henrietta everything.'

'I . . . I expect she seemed almost like a real person,' Ellie said.

Mrs Lloyd-Hughes nodded. 'That's exactly right, my dear. So do you understand now why I don't want to have anything to do with a toy museum? After losing Henrietta, I couldn't look at another doll without feeling ill, and even now I'd rather have nothing to do with the things.'

Sadly Ellie nodded that she *did* understand.

'I must say you seem like a very sympathetic little girl,' Mrs Lloyd-Hughes said. She looked thoughtful for a moment. Then she said, 'Do you see that bookcase over there? There's an old photograph album on the bottom shelf. Can you fetch it for me?'

Ellie did as she was asked. As soon as she handed over the album Mrs Lloyd-Hughes began leafing through it as if she was looking for something. It was full of black-and-white photos, and Ellie caught several glimpses of a baby in a frilly bonnet and two little boys in sailor suits. But it wasn't until the old lady reached a page with a photograph of a little girl on it that she stopped and allowed Ellie to look properly. Ellie saw that the little girl, who looked about the same age as herself, was standing stiffly against a mantelpiece, dressed in a frilly white smock and holding a china doll in the crook of one arm.

'That's me,' Mrs Lloyd-Hughes told her, 'and *that* is Henrietta.'

Ellie stared at the china doll. Apart from

her clothes, she looked remarkably like Enid. The face and hair seemed almost identical, although it was difficult to tell exactly because the photo was in black and white. 'Did Henrietta have blonde or dark hair?' Ellie asked.

'Blonde, of course! Can't you tell? I loved her hair – it was the real stuff, you know! Dolls often had real hair in those days – well, the *best* ones did.'

'And what colour was her dress?'

'It was a lovely bright yellow. She had matching knickers and knitted yellow bootees as well. You can't imagine how pretty she looked.' The old lady sighed, a faraway look in her eyes. 'I cried and cried when I came home that day and found her gone. My mother said that Henrietta had probably been given to some crippled child in an orphanage and that I should be glad about that. But how could I be glad when I missed her so much?'

Ellie was beginning to get an idea. The trouble was, it meant doing something dishonest. But on the other hand it wouldn't hurt anybody, and it might even make Mrs Lloyd-Hughes happy. Better still, it might actually save the toy museum.

As she heard her aunt announcing from the doorway that they really must be going now, Ellie said quickly, 'I'll put your album away for you before I go, shall I?'

And without waiting for a reply, she took the album from the old lady and carried it back to its bookcase, where she secretly removed the photograph of Henrietta and slipped it into her pocket.

6

The fairies had said they would meet Ellie at six o'clock that evening at the bottom of Aunt Megan's garden, where Ellie had hoped to be able to give them the news that Mrs Lloyd-Hughes had agreed to save the toy museum.

At six o'clock Ellie was waiting by the bottom fence just as they'd agreed, and it didn't take long for Myfanwy and Bronwen to appear.

'Well?' they demanded excitedly. 'How did it go?'

'Not *exactly* how we wanted it to,' Ellie

began, 'but I've had another idea . . .' And she explained her new plan to them, taking the photograph of Henrietta out of her pocket to show them.

'I'm not sure what Queen Lily will say, but we'll go and tell her straight away,' Bronwen promised.

'Take good care of this photograph, won't you?' Ellie said as she handed it to them.

'Of course we will,' Bronwen said. 'But even if Queen Lily agrees to try out your plan, it will take us at least a whole day to get everything ready, so we won't be able to bring it back to you until then. We'd better make it midnight tomorrow – that should give our fairy dressmakers all the time they need.'

And after they had chatted for a little longer, the fairies flew off over the fields, saying that they had to check quickly on the sheep with the poorly leg before they flew back to Fairyland.

When by the following afternoon Ellie still hadn't heard anything from the fairies, she took it as a sign that Queen Lily had agreed to try out her idea. Aunt Megan was taking Ellie and David to the cinema, and as they drove through the village Aunt Megan stopped her car outside the toy museum and said that she was just popping in to see Mr Daniels for a few minutes.

Ellie got out of the car and went with her.

'So how did it go at the solicitor's?' Aunt Megan wanted to know, as soon as Mr Daniels had invited them inside.

Ellie stayed in the office to listen as Mr Daniels told Aunt Megan that his solicitor had advised him to go ahead with the sale.

'I've also had an estate agent come over to take a look, and apparently it's a fair price I'm being offered for the place.'

'But couldn't you wait just a *bit* longer to see if you get any donations?' Ellie asked.

Aunt Megan looked at her, clearly surprised by her outspokenness. 'Ellie's become quite the little chatterbox in the last day or so,' she said. She went on to tell Mr Daniels about their visit to Mrs Lloyd-Hughes, though since Ellie hadn't told her aunt about Henrietta, all Aunt Megan knew was that the old lady had refused to help them because she didn't like toys.

'Well, I appreciate your efforts, Ellie,' Mr Daniels said, 'and if you have any other ideas, you let me know. I'd willingly have a shot at just about anything, if I thought it might save the museum. As it is, I reckon

I can only hold out for a few more days before I'll have to give up the fight.'

'It seems such a shame that *all* the toys have to go,' Aunt Megan said. 'I was thinking, Daniel – surely it couldn't hurt to keep a few for yourself?'

Mr Daniels sighed. 'The trouble is that this London fellow who's offering to buy the place is insisting on having the museum logbook included in the sale. It lists everything in the museum, and he was very clear that any offer he made must include every single toy. I think he suspects that some of the toys might be valuable and that I might try and diddle him out of the best ones.'

'Does the logbook tell you who *gave* each toy to the museum?' Ellie asked, thinking about Enid and her claim to have once belonged to the Queen.

'In most cases, yes,' Mr Daniels said. 'My father always wrote down the details of how and when each toy was acquired. Though since handwriting wasn't one of his strong points, I've never found it easy to read.'

'Do you think I could have a look at it?' Ellie asked.

'We haven't got time for that now, Ellie,' Aunt Megan said, glancing at her watch. 'We'd better go, if we want to get to the cinema in time.'

'OK, but I just want to have a quick look at the dolls first,' Ellie said, hurrying into the main room to look inside the cabinet that contained Enid and the others. Their clothes were back to normal – except that Enid's dress was no longer hitched up – and there was no sign of the fairies. Ellie stared for a few moments at Enid, trying to imagine her wearing clothes like the ones Henrietta had worn in Mrs Lloyd-Hughes's photograph. If they could just get the dress right, and comb her hair a little bit differently, then it *should* work, she thought, and she crossed her fingers for luck before rushing off to join her aunt.

Bronwen and Myfanwy had told Ellie not to try to stay awake that night as they would wake her up themselves when they arrived in her room.

'Well, don't you dare throw water over me,' she had told them, and they had promised that they wouldn't.

Instead of using water, the two fairies showered her with fairy dust, which tickled her nose and made her sneeze herself awake.

'Come on,' they said as soon as she opened her eyes. 'Queen Lily wants you to

come to the toy museum with us and see Enid for yourself!'

'I can't walk into the village at this time of night,' Ellie said, yawning.

'You won't have to. We've brought transport.'

'What sort of transport?'

'A pony. Normally he's just an ordinary Welsh pony, but tonight Queen Lily has used some very strong fairy dust to make him grow wings. He's always wanted to fly, so he's very excited about it. Come on. He's waiting for you outside the window.'

Thrilled, Ellie rushed to the window and there, hovering just beneath the window ledge, clearly visible in the moonlight, was the cutest Welsh pony she had ever seen. He had a glistening white coat with a cream mane and tail, and attached to both shoulders were the most enormous gold sparkly wings. The pony was flapping them up and down and swishing his tail proudly.

Ellie gasped. 'He looks a bit like a unicorn, but without the pointy bit on his head.'

'Unicorns are make-believe, silly!' Myfanwy exclaimed, giggling. 'Nobody in their right mind believes in *those*! Now climb on to his back and he'll take you to the museum!'

'Here, you'd better wear this so you don't get cold,' Bronwen said, handing her a child-sized knitted cape. It was yellow and glittery, with tiny daffodils embroidered all over it, and when Ellie put it on over her nightdress it fitted perfectly and felt wonderfully soft.

'It's lovely,' she said. 'Thank you.'

'Don't thank us. Thank the fairy dressmakers. It's made from the same wool they used to knit Enid's new bootees. You'll meet them when we get to the museum.'

Ellie could hardly believe she wasn't dreaming as she sat astride the flying pony, which took her high over the fields and rooftops towards the toy museum. The sky was clear and she could see the stars twinkling brightly above her as they flew. There was a coolish breeze, which made her grateful for the warm cape around her shoulders, and the fact that the pony's back was warm too. Bronwen was flying to one side of her while Myfanwy flew ahead, leading the way. The little pony whinnied with excitement every so often, as if *he* could hardly believe this was really happening either.

Finally they arrived at the museum, where the pony flew down to allow Ellie to climb straight on to the little landing at the top of the museum stairs. 'Thanks for the ride,' Ellie said, patting the pony's velvety nose after she had climbed off.

Bronwen and Myfanwy led the way inside, and when she entered the main room Ellie gasped in delight.

Fairy lights were strung up everywhere, and Enid, Llewellyn, Dilys and Tedi were all out of their cabinet. There were lots of fairies Ellie hadn't seen before, who all seemed to be gathered around something in the middle of the room. Some of them held needles and thread, others had pins in their mouths, some carried miniature tape measures and one was balancing a large pincushion on her head.

'These are the fairy dressmakers,' Bronwen told her.

As a few of the fairies moved out of the way, Ellie saw that the object they were gathered around was Enid. She was wearing a yellow frilly dress instead of her old blue one, and she was lifting up one foot for two fairies to tug a yellow bootee on to it.

'Enid looks . . . she looks . . .' Ellie began tentatively.

'Like Henrietta?' asked a familiar fairy voice, and Ellie turned to see the fairy queen flying towards her.

'Yes!' Ellie gasped. 'At least, I think so!

Has somebody got the photograph so we can check?'

Two fairies immediately flew forward and dropped it into her hand.

'These are two of our head fairy dressmakers.' Queen Lily introduced them. 'They have worked very hard to make Enid's outfit look exactly how it does in the photograph. They also designed your

new cape. I must say, it looks very pretty on you.'

'Oh, it *is* pretty – thank you *so* much,' Ellie quickly told the two fairies, who smiled and said that she was welcome.

'Both the cloak and Enid's new clothes are made from human materials, so they shouldn't arouse any suspicion when they are worn,' Queen Lily told her.

Suddenly Enid spoke up, sounding cross. 'I don't think yellow is my colour at all,' she complained, 'and these knickers are very scratchy. You've put far too much lace in them.'

'My fairies had to guess at the style of the knickers,' Queen Lily explained to Ellie, 'since they weren't visible in the photograph. But we thought since the dress was so fancy then the knickers would be as well. That's why we decided to trim them with lace. Of course, a lot of old dolls lose parts of their outfits over time, and we did wonder whether to dispense with the knickers entirely, but Enid was rather upset by that idea.'

'I have always worn knickers,' Enid declared haughtily, 'and as a doll that was once a part of the royal family, I think it most unseemly not to.'

Dilys, Tedi and Llewellyn, who had all been watching Enid's transformation from the comfort of the dolls' pram, began to snigger loudly.

'Regardless of whether Enid is correct in thinking she was once a royal doll, she is doing us all a great favour by agreeing to pose as Henrietta,' Queen Lily reminded them sternly.

As the toys did their best to look more serious, the fairy queen turned to Ellie and said, 'What we still have to work out is how we are going to get Mrs Lloyd-Hughes to come to the museum.'

'What if I show her a photograph of Enid dressed as Henrietta?' Ellie suggested. 'I could take it with David's digital camera. Then she's bound to want to come to the museum to actually *see* Enid – I mean, Henrietta – for herself. And with any luck, when she gets here she'll be so happy to see Henrietta again – and so horrified at the thought of her being sent away to London with the rest of the toys – that she'll give Mr Daniels a big enough donation to save the museum!'

'I'll go and fetch David's camera now,' Myfanwy said. 'I saw it on the dressing table when we went to collect you, Ellie. Don't worry, I'll be very careful not to wake him.' And she flew off.

'There is one other problem, Ellie,' Queen Lily said, frowning. 'Even if Mrs Lloyd-Hughes believes that the photograph you show her *is* Henrietta, in order for her to *continue* to believe that, we need Enid to remain in her new clothes permanently. But surely Mr Daniels will notice that her clothes are different.'

Ellie thought for a moment. 'I think we have to tell him the truth,' she said. 'Not about the fairy portal and all the toys coming to life ... but about Henrietta and my idea to make Mrs Lloyd-Hughes think that Enid is her doll. He said today that he'd do anything to save the museum – and if I point out how this would be the best thing for everyone – including Mrs Lloyd-Hughes – then I think he might agree.'

As soon as she had spoken, the toys

immediately started to discuss whether or not it was fair to ask Mr Daniels to do something that dishonest, and the fairies began to argue loudly among themselves about whether he was likely to help them or not. Queen Lily stayed silent, deep in thought.

They were still arguing when Myfanwy arrived back, dangling David's camera beneath her as she flew into the room.

Ellie quickly took it from her and announced as politely as she could, 'Can all you fairies please get out of the way so I can take a photograph of Enid?'

'Oh, don't worry – fairies don't show up in human photographs,' Myfanwy told her, deliberately flying over to join Enid.

So Ellie took a picture of Enid and Myfanwy together, and sure enough when she looked at the little screen on the back of the camera afterwards, Enid alone was in the frame.

'There isn't time for me to get a picture printed off,' Ellie said, 'but I can take the camera to Mrs Lloyd-Hughes's house tomorrow and let her look at it on the back. I'll return her photograph of Henrietta too. I just hope I can get it back inside the album without her seeing me.'

'Myfanwy and I will come and help you, if you like,' Bronwen offered.

'Thanks,' Ellie said, stifling a yawn.

'It's time we got Ellie back to bed,' Queen Lily announced. 'Bronwen, please go and tell our pony that we need him to fly Ellie home now.' She turned to Ellie. 'Bronwen and Myfanwy will help you as much as they can tomorrow. But as for the best way to deal with Mr Daniels . . . I think we must leave that up to you.'

7

The following morning Ellie slipped her brother's camera in her bag and went downstairs to tell her aunt she was going into the village to buy a comic.

'All right, Ellie. Maybe David wants to go with you.'

But fortunately for Ellie, David didn't. 'I'm going to go out by myself to do some sketches of the wildlife,' he told them. 'I might take some photographs too. Have you seen my camera, Ellie?'

'No,' Ellie lied, clutching her bag and willing herself not to look guilty.

'David had a strange dream about his camera last night,' Aunt Megan told Ellie. 'He was just telling me about it. He dreamt it was being carried through the air and out of the window.'

'Really?' Ellie was startled. 'Did you see *who* was carrying it?' she asked him.

David scowled. 'No. But it's no wonder I'm getting weird dreams, having to listen to all the nonsense *you* talk!'

Ellie realized that she'd better leave before David discovered that his camera really had been taken. 'See you later,' she said quickly to Aunt Megan, before hurrying through the door.

Bronwen and Myfanwy had promised to meet her outside the church at ten o'clock, and as soon as she got there they flew out from behind an old gravestone and greeted her excitedly.

'So what do you want us to do when we get there?' Bronwen asked as they headed towards Mrs Lloyd-Hughes's house together.

'I suppose the *main* thing is to get her attention away from me while I'm putting the photograph of Henrietta back in its album,' Ellie replied.

'That will be easy,' Myfanwy said, grinning. 'We can always knock an ornament off a shelf, or fly up to the ceiling and give one of the chandeliers a bit of a rattle – if there *are* any chandeliers, that is. Fewer and fewer houses seem to have them these days.'

'I don't want you to break anything,' Ellie said. 'Especially not her ornaments, because they look really expensive.'

'We could just tap on the window with a branch or something,' Bronwen suggested.

'But we'll have to stay outside to do that.'

'What if she sees you?' Ellie frowned. 'I mean, do you know for a fact that she doesn't believe in fairies?'

'Oh yes,' Myfanwy said confidently. 'Last summer a whole bunch of us gatecrashed one of her garden parties and she didn't see any of us – though one of her friends did, which was a bit tricky.'

They had reached the front door now and Ellie rang the bell. As she waited for the housekeeper to appear, the two fairies flew off to find some suitable twigs to bang against the living-room window.

'Wait until you see me pick up the photograph album before you do it,' Ellie called after them, and they nodded that they would, before disappearing into the garden.

*

The housekeeper led her straight into the living room, where Mrs Lloyd-Hughes was sitting reading a book. She looked up in astonishment when she saw who it was.

'Ellie? What a surprise! Is your aunt not with you this time?'

Feeling a wave of shyness come over her, Ellie swallowed and shook her head. Out of the corner of her eye she could see Myfanwy waiting outside the window, waving a large twig.

'I've got something to tell you,' she blurted. 'It's about Henrietta. I saw a doll that looks just like the one in that photograph you showed me, and I think it might be her. She's in the toy museum and I took a picture of her on my brother's camera. Look.'

Before Mrs Lloyd-Hughes had time to speak, Ellie had switched on the camera and was pressing the button that displayed all the stored images. She showed the old lady the picture of Enid dressed in Henrietta's clothes.

Mrs Lloyd-Hughes put on her reading glasses in order to see more clearly, then let out a shocked gasp. 'You're right! This looks exactly like her!'

'I know. That's why I thought I'd better come straight away to tell you.'

'Quick, pass me the photograph album again. I need to have another look at Henrietta,' the old lady instructed.

So Ellie went to the bookcase and, with her back still turned towards Mrs Lloyd-Hughes, she started to flick through the album herself, saying, 'I'll just find the right page for you, shall I?'

'I'll do that! Just bring it here!' the old lady snapped impatiently.

Flustered, Ellie dropped the photograph, but luckily at that moment there was a loud rattling sound on the window. Mrs Lloyd-Hughes turned to see what it was, which gave Ellie enough time to pick up the photograph again without being seen.

'What on earth . . . ?' Mrs Lloyd-Hughes was staring, mesmerized, as first a large leafy twig and then a red rose (which Bronwen must have taken from one of the flower beds) began to dance across the outside of the windowpane.

Ellie leafed through the book until she found the right page, slipped the photograph in the correct slot and shut the album again. Then she carried it over to the old lady, who was still staring open-mouthed at the window.

'It must be the wind,' Ellie said, and suddenly, as if they had heard her, the rose and the leafy twig both flopped to the ground.

'That's the strangest gust of wind *I've* ever seen,' Mrs Lloyd-Hughes muttered, finally turning back to look at Ellie. 'Oh, you've brought the album. Now let's see . . .'

She sat for a long time comparing both pictures before asking Ellie to fetch her magnifying glass from the bureau so that she could inspect them even more closely.

Finally, after what seemed like forever, Mrs Lloyd-Hughes sighed loudly and said, 'I must say I have to agree with you, Ellie. This doll does look like she might be my Henrietta. Her dress is a different shade of yellow to the way I remember it, but it's difficult to tell what colours are really like from a photograph. Do you think you could arrange for her to be brought to me? And I promise you, if this *is* Henrietta, your friend won't have to worry any more about not having enough money to keep his museum going. So long as he lets me have Henrietta back, I will give him all the money he requires.'

'Oh ...' Ellie hadn't expected Mrs Lloyd-Hughes to want to *keep* Enid, and she wasn't quite sure how to respond. 'W-wouldn't it be better if Henrietta stayed in the museum, where lots of people can admire her?' she pointed out nervously.

'Of course not! Do you really think that if I found Henrietta again after all this time, I'd want her to be anywhere but here in this house with *me*?'

'I . . . I suppose not,' Ellie admitted, telling herself that perhaps Enid wouldn't mind living with Mrs Lloyd-Hughes. Anyway, since she still had to convince the old lady that Enid *was* Henrietta when they met for real, she supposed it was a bit early to start worrying about what might happen afterwards.

Bronwen and Myfanwy were waiting for her when she got outside.

'She wants Mr Daniels to bring Enid to her, so I'll have to go and talk to him now and see what he says,' she told them.

They hurried towards the museum and on the way Ellie told them the rest of what Mrs Lloyd-Hughes had said.

'What?' Bronwen exclaimed when Ellie had told them everything. 'Do you mean she'd want Enid to actually *leave* the museum?'

'Yes,' Ellie said. 'Do you think she'll mind? It *is* a very comfortable house – much more comfortable than the toy museum – and—'

'She can't leave,' Bronwen interrupted. 'If Enid isn't there to sit around the picnic rug with the others, then the fairy portal can't exist. The portal needs all four toys in order for it to work.'

Ellie frowned in dismay. 'So for the fairy portal to work, none of those toys must leave the museum?'

Bronwen nodded.

Ellie couldn't help feeling frustrated with the fairies for only telling her about this now. 'Well, I don't know what else we can do,' she said flatly. 'Maybe Mr Daniels can persuade Mrs Lloyd-Hughes to let Enid stay at the museum, but I doubt it. In fact, he's far more likely to let her have anything she wants, if it means his museum gets saved. After all, *he* doesn't know about the fairy portal, does he?'

Myfanwy sounded upset. 'What are we going to do then?'

'I don't know,' Ellie replied. 'I guess the first thing is to tell Queen Lily what's happened.'

When they reached the museum they were greeted at the door by a very excited Mr Daniels.

'I've just had a phone call from Mrs Lloyd-Hughes, Ellie,' he said. 'She told me all about your visit. I had no idea that one of the dolls here once belonged to her. Anyway, she's asked if I'll show her the doll, on the understanding that if it *is* the same one she lost as a child, she'll pay me everything I need to keep the museum running, in exchange for getting her doll back. Isn't it wonderful? She says it's a china doll in a yellow dress.

What's puzzling is that I don't remember having a doll like that here, but she says *you* know which one she means.'

Ellie took a deep breath. 'Mr Daniels, there's something you need to know,' she began. 'You see, I really wanted to save the museum, so I did something I probably shouldn't have . . .' And she told him how she had tried to pass Enid off as Henrietta by dressing her like the doll in Mrs Lloyd-Hughes's photograph. (Though of course she didn't mention the help she had had from the fairies.)

'I don't understand,' Mr Daniels said. 'When exactly did you do this? And how could you open up the cabinet? And where did you get the yellow dress from?'

Ellie thought very quickly. 'I . . . I borrowed the key from your office while you were talking to Aunt Megan – and that's when

I did it. And . . . and the yellow dress came from . . . it came from one of my own dolls.'

'Really?' Mr Daniels sounded incredulous.

Ellie swallowed. She hated lying, but before she had time to say any more, a car pulled up outside.

To Ellie's amazement, Mrs Lloyd-Hughes's housekeeper got out of the car and went to open the back door.

'She's actually come here herself!' Ellie gasped as Mrs Lloyd-Hughes emerged.

'She did sound very excited on the phone,' Mr Daniels said, frowning as if he was deep in thought. 'Ellie, about this doll . . . is she still wearing the yellow dress?'

'Yes.'

'Then maybe we should let Mrs Lloyd-Hughes decide for herself whether the doll is hers or not.'

'But Mr Daniels, she's definitely *not* because—'

'You can't know that for sure,' he interrupted her. 'I mean, she could have had a change of clothes over the years. Maybe the doll we have here really *did* have a yellow dress originally. Anyway, if Mrs Lloyd-Hughes says she's the right doll, then that's good enough as far as I'm concerned. After all, what harm can it do?'

'That's what I thought at first,' Ellie said. 'But, Mr Daniels, now I don't think you *should* give Enid – I mean the china doll that's here – to Mrs Lloyd-Hughes. After all, she's . . . she's . . . a very special antique doll and she belongs in your museum!' If only she could explain about the fairy portal, she thought desperately. But she knew he would never believe her even if she did.

Unfortunately Mr Daniels had a strange,

determined sort of look on his face. 'Beggars can't be choosers, Ellie,' he said firmly. 'At least this way I'm only sacrificing *one* doll for the sake of all the rest. And like I told you before, I'm willing to do just about anything to save my museum.'

And before Ellie could say anything else Mr Daniels was on his way down the steps to meet Mrs Lloyd-Hughes, who was prodding the wooden staircase with her walking stick as if she suspected that it might collapse at any minute.

Bronwen and Myfanwy had already gone inside the museum. Ellie quickly followed them and found the four toys sitting around the little picnic rug, still inside their cabinet. The rug was glowing brightly and Bronwen and Myfanwy were hovering above it, getting ready to fly back through the fairy portal.

'We have to go and tell Queen Lily what's happening straight away,' Bronwen called out to her, as bright rays of light began to shoot out from the rug.

'But, Ellie, you mustn't let that old lady take Enid away from here! If she does, none of the other fairies who are out in the valley today will be able to get home to Fairyland!' Myfanwy warned her in a frightened voice, as both fairies flew into the light and disappeared.

Fortunately Mrs Lloyd-Hughes took a very long time to climb up the stairs, which gave Ellie time to think. She had to stop Enid being taken from the museum, at least until all the valley fairies had a chance to get home through the fairy portal. But how was she going to do it?

Suddenly she remembered that the cabinets were all locked and that she had seen the keys hanging up in Mr Daniels's office.

She got to the office just as Mr Daniels and Mrs Lloyd-Hughes were nearing the

top of the stairs. There was a bunch of small keys that opened the cabinets, and Ellie quickly snatched it from its peg and shoved it into her pocket. Then she rushed back into the little lobby area.

'Hello, Mrs Lloyd-Hughes,' Ellie said, as cheerfully as possible, when the old lady stepped in through the door.

'Hello, Ellie. After your visit I decided that I had to come and see this doll straight away.'

'She's through here,' Ellie said, 'though I'm not so sure now that she really *is* the same one. You see—'

'I shall know if it is Henrietta, don't you worry,' the old lady interrupted, stepping past Ellie into the main room while Mr Daniels followed behind.

The old lady headed straight for the central cabinet. The toys were still sitting around the rug, although they were all completely motionless now and Ellie couldn't tell if they were aware of what was happening or not.

'Well?' Mr Daniels asked, sounding a bit hesitant. '*Is* she yours, do you think?'

Mrs Lloyd-Hughes had tears in her eyes as she stared at Enid. 'The dress is unmistakable – though the colour has faded somewhat. Her face is more or less how I remember it. Her hair is perhaps a little different – but then my memory cannot be perfect after all this time.'

'If your memory's not perfect, hadn't you better take some time to think about it?' Ellie said quickly.

'What good will thinking about it do?' the old lady retorted. 'I should like to examine her more closely, Mr Daniels. Will you take her out of the cabinet for me?'

'Of course. I'll go and get the key.'

Ellie felt her stomach start to churn as she waited with Mrs Lloyd-Hughes, and it seemed like an eternity later when Mr Daniels returned with a puzzled look on his face. 'I can't find the cabinet keys. I've searched all over the office and they're not there.' He looked suspiciously at Ellie. 'You said you borrowed them before. You haven't still got them, have you?'

Ellie flushed as she shook her head, hoping he wouldn't ask to search her pockets.

'I might have left them in here somewhere,' Mr Daniels told the old lady. 'If you can wait for a few minutes, I'll have a look round.'

Ten minutes later Mrs Lloyd-Hughes was getting extremely impatient. 'If I can't examine the doll properly, then I can't confirm that she's Henrietta,' she said crossly. 'Surely you can't be so incompetent as to have lost *all* the keys? Don't you have a spare set somewhere?'

Ellie's heart skipped a beat, but fortunately Mr Daniels muttered that he didn't know exactly where to lay his hands on the spare set. Flustered, he apologized and said that if Mrs Lloyd-Hughes wanted to go home and wait, then when he found the missing keys he would bring the doll straight to her.

Mrs Lloyd-Hughes, though clearly furious, had no choice but to do as he suggested.

When Mr Daniels returned after seeing the old lady to her car, Ellie produced the keys from her pocket straight away. 'I'm sorry, but I just didn't want her to take that doll away when I *know* she isn't Henrietta,' she told him.

Mr Daniels sighed, but he didn't look as cross as she'd expected. 'To tell you the truth, I felt bad about tricking her too,' he said. 'But I just didn't know what else to do.'

'Well,' Ellie began slowly, 'I *do* have another idea.'

'Come on then.' Mr Daniels sounded hopeful. 'Tell me what it is.'

Ellie had been thinking a lot about Enid's claim to have once belonged to the Queen. She knew the other toys thought Enid was making it up, but what if they were wrong? What if Enid really *had* belonged to the Queen? Surely that would mean they could ask the Queen to help them save the museum? Not that she could tell Mr Daniels what Enid had said. 'I think we should try to contact some of the people – or the sons and daughters of the people – who gave these toys to the museum in the first place,' she told Mr Daniels. 'Maybe one of them will want to help us. You did say you had their details in the museum logbook, didn't you?'

Mr Daniels looked doubtful about her plan, but he agreed to let Ellie see the logbook, which turned out to be a large, flat, leather-bound ledger that was as old as the museum itself. It was kept on the highest shelf in the museum office, and Mr Daniels had to use his set of folding steps to reach it.

'Fifty years ago, when my father started the museum, he bought this book so he could keep a record of all the toys,' Mr Daniels said, opening the logbook at the first page. 'The first entries are dated before the museum opened, because my father collected a lot of toys before he actually bought this place.' He smiled. 'I remember how excited he was about moving here. You see, legend has it that this building was erected on a piece of land where the village well once stood, and that it was no ordinary well but a magic one. It was said that some of the magic stones from the well were included in this building. Of course, it's probably just a lot of old nonsense, but my parents always believed it. My mother used to say that the house was a lucky house because of it – and that meant our museum would be lucky too.'

'Mr Daniels?' Ellie's attention had been caught by the old-fashioned spindly writing in the logbook. 'How can you *read* any of this?' There was no way she could make out Enid's name, or the name of any other toy for that matter.

'The best person to decipher that is my

mother,' Mr Daniels said. 'She's always been better than me at reading my father's handwriting.'

'Your mother's still *alive*?'

Mr Daniels grinned. 'Why? Did you think I was too old to have a mother who's still living? She's ninety-eight and she lives in the village nursing home. We can go and see her now, if you like.' He glanced quickly at his watch. 'Yes, I don't see why I shouldn't close the place for an hour or so. After all, it's not as if we've got a queue of visitors waiting outside, is it?'

'Mr Daniels, does your museum *ever* get any visitors?' Ellie couldn't help asking.

Mr Daniels smiled in a resigned sort of way. 'We usually get a steady trickle of tourists during the summer, and the local school sometimes brings classes here during term-time. But the museum doesn't bring

in a lot of money these days, I'm afraid. It
was much more popular in the old days.
Look – that's a photograph of the museum
on its tenth anniversary. Look at all the
visitors we had then!' He was pointing at
an old black-and-white photograph in a
frame on the wall, which Ellie hadn't
noticed until that moment.

'The museum looked exactly the same
then as it does now!' Ellie exclaimed.

'My mother made me promise not to
change things too much,' Mr Daniels
explained. 'She especially didn't ever want
me to change anything in that central cabinet, I remember. It was her idea to sit those
toys around the rug like that, as if they were
having a picnic.'

'Wow!' Ellie gasped, because sure enough,
if you looked closely, you could see Enid,
Tedi, Dilys and Llewellyn sitting around

the same rug in the same cabinet that they occupied today.

Just then the telephone rang, and to Ellie's surprise it turned out to be Aunt Megan.

'How did you know I was here?' Ellie asked her aunt, after Mr Daniels had handed her the phone.

'I guessed! But you really should have rung me to let me know you weren't coming straight home, Ellie.'

'Sorry,' Ellie mumbled. 'Aunt Megan, is it OK if I go and visit Mr Daniels's mother now? I want to ask her about some of the old toys.'

'I suppose so. I must say that for a girl who's meant to be shy, you seem to have become extremely sociable all of a sudden! Oh, and Ellie, have you seen David's camera? He can't find it anywhere.'

'Maybe his dream was real after all,' Ellie blurted, before quickly adding, 'I've got to go now, Aunt Megan. I'll see you later, OK?'

As she came off the phone, Mr Daniels was putting on his outdoor jacket. 'We won't be able to keep Mrs Lloyd-Hughes waiting forever,' he reminded her.

'I know,' Ellie said. 'But I still want to see if your mother can help us first. Do you think we can take that old photograph with us to show her? It might help her remember the toys and where they came from.' Ellie already had a photograph of Enid saved on David's camera, but it showed Enid in her new yellow dress rather than her old blue one, which Ellie thought might confuse the old lady.

'I don't see why not, but before we go, you have to promise not to tell my mother that I might have to sell the museum,' Mr Daniels replied. 'She doesn't know anything about it yet, and goodness knows *what* she'd say if she thought that my father's whole collection of toys was going to be sent to London for some spoilt little rich girl to play with.'

'Don't worry, Mr Daniels. I'm getting very good at keeping secrets,' Ellie assured him as she followed him outside, carrying the logbook very carefully under one arm and the old picture of the museum just as carefully under the other.

9

The nursing home was situated on the edge of the village in the opposite direction from Aunt Megan's house. Mr Daniels said that since the sun was shining his mother would probably be sitting outside in her wheel-chair so, after they had signed the visitors book in the hall, he led the way straight through to the back garden.

Several old people were sitting outside and some of them had visitors or a nurse sitting with them.

'There she is,' Mr Daniels said, leading Ellie towards a tiny old lady, wearing large round spectacles, who was sitting in her wheelchair on the patio.

The old lady looked delighted to see him, and she gave Ellie a big smile when her son introduced her. She looked very wrinkly and extremely frail, but that wasn't surprising since she was almost a hundred years old, Ellie thought.

'Ellie wanted to come and see you because she's very interested in our toy museum,' he told his mother. 'We were trying to read Dad's logbook, but I couldn't make out his writing. I told Ellie you'd probably be able to help us.'

'Of course I can! Now what is it you want to know, my dear?' Mrs Daniels asked Ellie.

'I'd like to know where some of the toys came from,' Ellie began shyly. 'There's one toy in particular – a china doll – that I'd really like you to look up in the logbook. I've brought this old photograph to show you. That's her there – the china doll in the cabinet with the other toys. See?'

'Ah . . . now . . . I can still remember the day that picture was taken,' the old lady said with a wistful sigh as she peered through her glasses at the old photograph. 'The china doll is Enid . . . and that's Dilys, Tedi and Llewellyn, all sitting around the rug with her.'

'I didn't know you gave any of the toys names, Mam.' Mr Daniels sounded surprised.

'Oh, *I* didn't name them,' the old lady said, giving Ellie a knowing look. 'They chose those names themselves.'

Ellie stared in surprise at Mrs Daniels, suddenly wondering if she knew about the fairies and how they were able to make the toys in the museum come to life.

Mr Daniels was looking a little worried, as if he thought his mother's mind might not be as sound as he had previously thought. 'Are you feeling all right, Mam?' he asked. 'The sun's not too strong for you, is it?'

Mrs Daniels smiled at her son and quickly asked him to show her the logbook, which he placed on her lap and opened at the first page. 'Some dolls keep the names their owners give them,' she told Ellie. 'In that case, the name will be in the logbook. But if I remember correctly that *wasn't* the case for any of those toys ... Now ... I think Dilys and Tedi were two of the first toys we were given, just after the museum opened.' She stopped at the bottom of the first page and bent her head down closer to the book in order to read the spindly writing. 'Here we are. They came to the museum together. They're listed here as "Welsh costume doll" and "teddy bear". They were both donated fifty years ago by the local vicar who was leaving to go and work in another parish. He was moving out of the vicarage and he found some toys in the loft that he said had been put there just after his wife died twenty years before. She had been collecting things for a church sale apparently, only the sale never happened because she got ill. After she died he couldn't face sorting through all the stuff she had collected, so he shoved it all out of the way up in his loft – and there it stayed for the next twenty years! Tedi and Dilys were among those things.'

'So I suppose you never knew who their original owners were?' Ellie said.

'No. Twenty years is a long time. I suppose Tedi and Dilys's original owners were quite grown-up by then. But it was the china doll you especially wanted to know about, wasn't it? Now let me think . . . I believe it was Mr Owen from the garage who brought her to the museum — along with Llewellyn, the wooden soldier.'

'I've met Mr Owen already!' Ellie exclaimed. She was about to add that he was a good friend of the fairies, but decided against it since Mr Daniels looked confused enough as it was.

'It was when he was very young man, just after his father died, I think . . .' the old lady continued. 'That must have been a year or two after we opened the museum. He found the toy soldier when he was clearing out his father's things. I believe the china doll belonged to a young lady he was courting at the time. I don't have any more information than that — but you can always go and speak to him yourself if you want to know more.'

'Was . . . was the girl he was courting a member of the royal family, by any chance?' Ellie couldn't help asking.

Mr Daniels and his mother burst out laughing.

'I don't think so, or it would have been the talk of the whole village,' the old lady replied, smiling. 'But why don't you go and ask him – I expect he'll be tickled pink at the idea!' She paused for a moment. 'Now tell me, Ellie . . . why all these questions about the toys?'

But before Ellie could reply, Mr Daniels jumped in, saying, 'She's just very interested in the history of old dolls, isn't that right, Ellie?'

Ellie nodded and did her best to smile innocently.

Mrs Daniels was looking at her curiously.

'Well, that's very nice. So you like dolls a lot, do you, Ellie?'

'Oh yes, I love them!' Ellie replied. 'Especially the ones in your museum.'

'And have you many dolls of your own?'

'Quite a few. My favourite is a rag doll called Trixie.'

'And do you have any . . . what you might call . . . *antique* dolls?'

Ellie shook her head. 'My granny had a beautiful china doll that I really loved and I thought she might give her to me, but she gave her to my cousin instead because she's the oldest grandchild.' Ellie had been quite sad about that, especially since her cousin didn't like dolls nearly as much as she did.

'I see.' The old lady looked thoughtful. 'Perhaps you might come and see me another time, Ellie. And if you come on your own, we can have a nice *girlie* chat. How about that?'

'What's a *girlie* chat?' Mr Daniels wanted to know.

'Oh – it's when we talk about things you wouldn't be interested in, Daniel. About . . . oh . . . princesses and mermaids and *fairies* and the like . . . Isn't that right, Ellie?'

Ellie stared at the old lady, certain now that she *had* met the fairies. She was longing to know more, but she knew she couldn't ask any further questions while Mr Daniels was with them.

'I'll come and see you again soon, Mrs Daniels,' she promised. First though, she had to go and see Mr Owen and find out once and for all whether Enid really *had* belonged to the Queen.

*

The first thing Ellie did when Mr Daniels dropped her off at Aunt Megan's front gate was to delete the photos she had taken on David's camera. She had a problem, she realized now. How was she going to return the camera without David guessing that she had had it all along?

'Need some help?' asked a familiar fairy voice, and suddenly Myfanwy appeared from behind the hedge, closely followed by Bronwen.

'Myfanwy! Bronwen! I thought you weren't going to come to the valley any more, in case you got stuck here!'

'As soon as we saw the fairy portal was still working, we knew you must have stopped Enid from being taken, so Queen Lily asked us to come back and round up all the fairies who are still out in the valley. They're all on their way back to

the museum now, and we're meant to
with them, but we thought we'd come and
see how you were getting on first.'

Ellie quickly told them about David's
camera.

'Leave it to us,' Myfanwy said, flying
down and grabbing it from her. '*We'll* give it
back. You never know – if we do it properly
it might be enough to make him believe in
fairies again!'

ZX100

Ellie watched the two fairies disappear through an open window on the top floor, then made her way inside the house, to find Aunt Megan in the kitchen decorating a batch of fairy cakes.

Almost immediately she had an idea. 'I'd really like to take one of those cakes to Mr Owen, Aunt Megan,' she gushed. 'He was so kind, giving me that flower bracelet and the chocolate! And I bet he really likes fairy cakes, since he believes in fairies!'

Aunt Megan turned to smile at her. 'That's a very nice idea, Ellie. I don't see why we shouldn't give some away. Maybe Mr Daniels would like some as well, even though he *doesn't* believe in fairies. What do you think?'

Ellie nodded and started to tell her aunt about her visit to Mr Daniels's mother. 'Maybe we could take *her* some cakes too,' she suggested.

'Well, why don't you make some more, Ellie? I've got enough ingredients left over for at least another batch. Then you can give them to whoever you think would like them.'

'Oh, but I'd like to go and visit Mr Owen now,' Ellie said quickly.

Just then David yelled out, 'ELLIE!' from the top of the stairs, so Ellie left Aunt Megan putting the chocolate buttons and sparkly sprinkles on to her cakes and headed up to their bedroom.

David was sitting on his bed, looking as if he had just seen a ghost. His camera was lying on the bed beside him and there was no sign of Myfanwy or Bronwen.

'I just saw . . .' he began, and his voice was trembling slightly. 'I mean, I *think* I just saw . . .'

'Did you see a fairy?' Ellie asked him

excitedly, hardly able to believe that her brother could now see fairies too.

David nodded, looking nervous. 'Maybe it was a trick of the light.'

'Of course it wasn't! I told you – there really *are* fairies here, but you can only see them if you believe in them.'

'But I *don't* believe in them!' David protested.

'Once a believer, always a believer!' a little voice called out, and this time it was clear that David could hear the voice too. Then Myfanwy flew out from behind the wardrobe and added, 'You believed in fairies once, you see, so when you saw your camera flying through the air just now, your *belief* in fairies – even though you'd completely forgotten you had any – was reawakened by your *disbelief* that a camera could fly on its own! So that's why you saw me!'

David was staring at her, completely stunned.

Myfanwy was so pleased that she did a loop-the-loop in mid-air. 'I'm the fairy you saved when I fell into the fishpond! Do you remember that now?'

Slowly David nodded. 'I . . . I think I'm starting to.'

Bronwen, who had been standing on the window ledge watching, flew over to Ellie and whispered in her ear that they should leave David and Myfanwy alone for a little while to get reacquainted.

Ellie went back downstairs to the kitchen (with Bronwen flying at her side) and they found Aunt Megan putting two fairy cakes in a little food container and pressing on the lid. 'Is David all right?' she asked Ellie. 'He's been very upset since he lost his camera.'

'Oh, he's just found it again,' Ellie said matter-of-factly.

'Really? Where?'

'Oh, just in his bedroom somewhere . . . Aunt Megan, is it OK if I go to the garage now to visit Mr Owen? I know how to get there and it's not that far.'

'I don't want you walking all that way on your own, Ellie,' Aunt Megan said. 'Help me clear up here first, and I'll come with you. Now, did you have anything to eat with Mr Daniels?'

Ellie had forgotten all about lunch, what with everything that had happened.

'There wasn't really time,' she admitted, so Aunt Megan insisted that Ellie sit down and eat a cheese sandwich before they set off to visit Mr Owen.

By the time she had finished it (with Bronwen helping by taking tiny bites of the cheese) David had arrived downstairs with Myfanwy. Aunt Megan asked about his camera and he grinned apologetically and said that it had been in his room the whole time. And before their aunt could ask any more questions Ellie told her brother that she wanted to go to see Mr Owen, and suggested *he* take her.

'Sure,' he agreed immediately, seeming to guess that the visit to Mr Owen had something to do with the fairies.

'Well, I don't know ...' Aunt Megan began uncertainly. 'I don't like the idea of the two of you going off by yourselves and arguing the whole way there and back.'

'It's OK, Aunt Megan, we won't argue!' they both assured her.

'Well, all right, then, but don't stay too long. Here – take these with you, Ellie.' And she handed Ellie the little container of fairy cakes for Mr Owen.

David couldn't help noticing that Myfanwy was staring longingly at the remaining fairy cakes on the table – in particular at a cake with pink icing and two chocolate buttons on the top.

'I don't suppose *we* could have a fairy cake each to eat on the way, could we, Aunt Megan?' he asked politely.

And both fairies beamed delightedly as Aunt Megan invited the children to help themselves.

On the way to the garage, Ellie told David all about the toy museum and the fairy portal. David listened incredulously while the fairies munched away at a chocolate button each, occasionally chipping in when they thought Ellie had missed out something important.

'So I want to ask Mr Owen if he knows where Enid really came from,' Ellie finished breathlessly. 'I mean, I know it's not very likely that she really *did* once belong to the Queen, but I don't think we should rule anything out.'

155

David gave a wry smile. 'Sure. I mean if *fairies* are real, and *toys* can come to life . . .' He shrugged vaguely as if he was still in a bit of a daze.

'Exactly. And if Enid *did* belong to the Queen, then maybe the Queen will help us to save the museum,' Ellie added. 'After all, *she* must have *lots* of money! And I don't suppose she'd want Enid back, because I'm sure the Queen must have lots of dolls – not like poor Mrs Lloyd-Hughes.'

When they got to the garage Mr Owen greeted them warmly, clearly delighted to see the two fairies. 'What can I offer you today, my dears? Some chocolate raisins perhaps?'

'Thank you, Mr Owen, but what we *really* need is your help with a question we've got for you,' Bronwen answered politely.

'But if you want to throw in a few

chocolate raisins as well then that would be great!' Myfanwy added, licking her lips greedily as her gaze fell on the sweet counter.

'Mr Owen, we're trying to find out who owned some of the old toys before they were given to the museum,' Ellie told him. 'Mrs Daniels told us it was *you* who donated Llewellyn and Enid. Is that right?'

'Llewellyn and Enid?' Mr Owen sounded puzzled.

'Llewellyn's a toy soldier and Enid's a china doll,' Ellie explained. 'I guess you might not have known their names.'

'I did give a wooden soldier to the museum many years ago, that's true,' Mr Owen said. 'I had to clear out my father's house after he died, and that's when I came across that toy soldier in his desk. He must have had it since he was a boy. I think I remember him showing it to me once and telling me it was too old to be played with.'

'Toys are never too old to be played with,' Myfanwy interrupted. 'That's why *we* always play with the ones in the museum whenever we can.'

'Oh well, you fairies should have told that to my father,' Mr Owen said. 'You could have, you know, because he believed in fairies too, though he was always so sad after my mother passed away when I was a boy that even the fairies couldn't cheer him up again. Anyhow, later I found another of those old toy soldiers. It had fallen down the back of one of the drawers inside his desk. I kept meaning to give that one to the museum too, only I never got round to it. I've still got it somewhere, I think.'

'What about the doll?' Ellie prompted him, because after all, it was Enid she was most interested in discovering the truth about.

'Ah yes ... the china doll ... Well, she wasn't mine. I handed her in on behalf of a young lady I was seeing at the time. Old Mr Daniels paid a bit of money for her, which my friend was very pleased to have because she'd just lost her job. She worked as a nanny, and when the family moved to London, they said they didn't need her any more. They paid her to help with the removal though, and after all the furniture vans had gone she found that china doll out in the garden. Apparently the little girl my friend looked after used to like pretending she was the Queen and that she was holding royal garden parties out in the garden! I suppose she must have forgotten that she'd left the doll out there.'

'So *that's* why Enid thinks she belonged to the Queen!' Ellie exclaimed.

Mr Owen looked puzzled. 'I beg your pardon?'

'It doesn't matter,' Ellie said swiftly. 'Go on, Mr Owen. What happened then?'

'Well, my girlfriend wrote to her employers asking if she should send the doll on to them,' Mr Owen continued, 'but they wrote back telling her not to bother as their daughter had plenty of dolls. So I spoke to old Mr Daniels about it and that's how we ended up taking her to the museum.'

'Do you know the name of that family, or where they moved to in London?' Ellie asked, thinking that if the little girl had grown up and was rich, then she might be willing to help them, even if she wasn't the Queen.

'I'm afraid not. My friend left the village

shortly afterwards when she got another
nannying job, and we lost touch after that.
She may have mentioned their name and
where they moved to – but if she did I can't
remember.'

After they had given Mr Owen his fairy
cakes and left the garage Ellie sighed loudly,
because it seemed like they had drawn a
complete blank.

'I don't know what to do now,' she said
gloomily.

'We'd better be getting back,' said
Bronwen, 'before Queen Lily starts wondering where we are.'

'We'll come with you to the museum
then,' Ellie said.

Twenty minutes later, while the fairies
took David into the museum room to
introduce him to the toys Ellie went
to speak to Mr Daniels, who was sitting in

his office staring guiltily at his desk.

'Mr Daniels, what's happened?' Ellie asked immediately, because she was certain that *something* had.

'I may as well tell you straight away, I suppose,' Mr Daniels said. 'Mrs Lloyd-Hughes rang me when I got back from visiting my mother. She wanted to know if I'd found the key to the dolls' cabinet yet. She said that her offer still stood if the doll turned out to be Henrietta.'

'Mr Daniels . . . you didn't . . . ?'

'I'm sorry, Ellie, but I decided to take the doll to her house so she could have a look at it. She examined it very carefully and at first she said that she couldn't be a hundred per cent sure if it was Henrietta or not. Apparently the doll's knickers weren't the same ones she remembered or something. But then she said that the dress itself was definitely the same and that maybe the knickers had been replaced at some point. Eventually she said that she was *almost* certain it was the doll she had lost and that she wanted to keep her in any case. She gave me a cheque for the museum there and then. And she said she was so happy she didn't mind if I chose *not* to change the name of the museum to reflect her donation!'

Ellie felt her knees go shaky as she realized they had arrived at the museum too late. The portal was gone – and with it, the only way for Bronwen and Myfanwy to return to Fairyland.

'But, Mr Daniels, this is terrible—' she gasped.

'It's not *that* terrible, surely?' he interrupted her. 'I mean, Mrs Lloyd-Hughes is happy, isn't she? And the museum is saved.'

'Oh – this is all my fault!' Ellie burst out. And before Mr Daniels could say any more she rushed through to the museum room.

Just as she had feared, Myfanwy and Bronwen were staring at the empty space in the cabinet where Enid had previously been. David was standing in the middle of the room looking bewildered, and several other fairies were hovering in the air looking frightened. Clearly it wasn't just Myfanwy and Bronwen who were trapped here.

'What are we going to do, Ellie?' Bronwen asked in a shaky voice as she entered the room.

'Ellie, you've *got* to get Enid back!' Myfanwy cried out. 'If you don't, we'll never see Fairyland again!'

Ellie knew then that there was only one thing she could do – she would have to go and see Mrs Lloyd-Hughes and tell her the truth.

She set off straight away, declining

David's offer to accompany her. This was something she knew she had to do on her own, and as soon as she reached Mrs Lloyd-Hughes's house she rang the bell and waited nervously for the housekeeper to appear. This time, to Ellie's surprise, the housekeeper was very friendly indeed as she invited Ellie inside. 'Mrs Lloyd-Hughes is a changed person since you found that old doll of hers,' she told Ellie. 'You take a seat in the living room, my love, and I'll tell her you're here.'

Mrs Lloyd-Hughes walked into the room a few minutes later, leaning on her stick and carrying Enid in her free arm. 'I must say I feel years younger, now that I've got my Henrietta back,' she told Ellie, giving her a beaming smile. 'You're a very kind girl for helping me!'

Ellie blushed. 'I'm afraid I'm not a kind

girl at all,' she said in a small voice. 'That's what I've come to tell you. You see, I tricked you.' And she waited for the old lady to sit down before telling her everything (excluding the part about the fairies being involved, of course).

When Ellie had finished talking, Mrs Lloyd-Hughes had a strange look on her face. Her wrinkled hand shook a little as she held on tightly to the doll in her lap. 'So what you're saying is that this doll wasn't actually wearing this dress when you first saw her in the museum?'

'No. She was wearing a blue dress – and it wasn't anything like the one in your photograph.'

'Still . . .' Mrs Lloyd-Hughes spoke sharply, 'clothes can change over the years. Her face and hair are the same, after all.'

'Her hair falls more on to her face

than Henrietta's in the photograph,' Ellie pointed out. 'And her parting is more to one side, whereas—'

'Hairstyles can change on dolls as well as on humans!' Mrs Lloyd-Hughes snapped. 'The important thing is that this doll *feels* like Henrietta! In any case, I have paid a lot of money for her and she belongs to me now!'

And to Ellie's dismay she found herself banished from the house and told never to come back.

That night Ellie couldn't get to sleep because she was thinking so much about Myfanwy and Bronwen and the other fairies who were having to spend their first night away from Fairyland. The toys would be awake too, and keeping them company in the museum, but that didn't change the fact that the fairies must be very frightened. And Queen Lily must be terribly worried about them, Ellie thought.

David sounded like he was tossing and turning in the bed next to her and eventually she whispered his name to see if he was awake.

'What is it?' he whispered back.

'I wish I could think of some way to help the fairies,' Ellie said, 'but without Enid the fairy portal just won't work.'

David didn't say anything for a few moments. Then he murmured, 'Does it have to be Enid who's the fourth toy? I mean, can't we just replace her with a different one?'

'Only certain toys can be part of the portal,' Ellie told him. 'And no other toy in the museum will do.'

'What about a toy that *isn't* in the museum?' David suggested.

'But how would we find one whose maker believed in fairies and whose first owner believed in fairies as well?' Ellie pointed out. 'I mean, I suppose we could try and find another really old toy and test it out, but – OH!' She suddenly sat up in bed and turned on the light.

'What are you doing?' David complained, rubbing his eyes.

'I've just remembered something! Mr Owen told us he had another toy soldier, didn't he? It belonged to his father, who definitely believed in fairies, and it must have had the same toymaker as Llewellyn! So if we put *him* in the portal, it might work again!'

Ellie woke up at seven o'clock the following morning and immediately felt excited as she remembered her plan.

'Come on,' she urged her brother, as she leapt out of bed. 'We've got to go and see Mr Owen again as soon as the garage opens!'

Luckily Aunt Megan didn't object when the children announced that they were going to visit Mr Owen straight after breakfast, but she was curious to know why they wanted to spend so much time with him all of a sudden.

'We just really like him,' Ellie said quickly. 'And . . . and he's got lots of stories to tell us about the fairies.'

'And you like to hear these stories as well, do you, David?' Aunt Megan asked, sounding surprised.

'Well . . . not exactly . . .' David murmured, flushing.

But before Aunt Megan could ask any more questions they had finished their breakfasts and were out through the door.

As soon as they arrived at the garage Ellie asked Mr Owen if he would be willing to give the second toy soldier he had told them about to the museum. 'The fairies need him, you see,' she explained. 'I can't tell you any more than that or I'd be giving away a fairy secret, but they really need him in order for their magic to work.'

'I'll do anything I can to help the fairies,' Mr Owen said immediately, and to Ellie's relief he didn't ask any questions. 'I'll go and have a look for that toy soldier straight away if you like – just so long as you two stay here and man the pumps for me.'

It took Mr Owen half an hour to return with the soldier – during which time David had served three customers. The soldier looked almost identical to Llewellyn, and the children thanked Mr Owen and felt very excited as they set off for the toy museum.

They got there to find Mr Daniels talking to someone on the phone in his office. As he paused to see what she wanted, Ellie quickly showed him the toy soldier and asked if she could put him in the case with the other toys. Mr Daniels nodded, taking the bunch of keys from its hook and giving it to her before returning to his call.

The two children hurried through to the museum room, where Bronwen immediately appeared, closely followed by Myfanwy.

'Are you all right?' Ellie asked them.

'Yes – though we're very hungry. I don't suppose you've brought us any of those fairy cakes, have you?'

Ellie shook her head apologetically. But if her plan worked, then hopefully the fairies would soon be able to enjoy a nice breakfast back in Fairyland.

'We've found another toy soldier,' David said. 'Show them, Ellie.'

'He looks exactly like Llewellyn!'

Bronwen exclaimed as Ellie held him up for the fairies to see.

'I know. Maybe they're brothers — if toy soldiers *have* brothers,' Ellie said. 'Anyway, we're hoping that if we put him with the other three toys, then the fairy portal might work again.'

Several other fairies flew into view now, as Ellie unlocked the door of the central cabinet. Llewellyn, Dilys and Tedi were sitting inside, looking just like ordinary toys, as she carefully placed the new soldier down beside them.

'I'll sprinkle some more fairy dust on them,' Bronwen said. 'The last lot must have worn off.' And she flew just above the toys and rubbed her fingers together until a very fine sparkly gold dust fell in a shower on to their heads.

Gradually, one by one, the toys started

to move – first Dilys, then Tedi and finally Llewellyn. The new soldier wasn't moving, Ellie noticed, but Bronwen told her not to worry. 'It always takes a bit longer for a toy who's never been brought to life before,' she explained. When Llewellyn saw the new toy soldier he let out a delighted gasp. 'It's one of my regiment! How wonderful! Where did you find him?' Ellie explained about Mr Owen and how his father had once owned both soldiers. As she spoke, the second soldier's eyes

suddenly seemed more alive. Then his feet
moved slightly. Then his head moved to
one side and finally his mouth creaked
open and he spoke. 'I say
– where the dickens am I?'

The other toys all
started to laugh
because he did have
a very strange way
of speaking.

'You're in the
toy museum,'
Llewellyn told him.

The newcomer
turned to look at
Llewellyn, clearly
relieved to see
another soldier. 'Has
the regiment been
posted here then?'

'I'm afraid we're the only ones left,' Llewellyn replied. 'The museum is a sort of retirement home for old toys like us. My name is Llewellyn, and these are my friends, Dilys and Tedi.'

'Very pleased to meet you, old chap,' the soldier said, giving Llewellyn a stiff salute, then reaching out to shake Dilys's hand and Tedi's paw. 'I am . . .' He paused, looking a little uncomfortable. 'Actually, I don't believe I *have* a name.'

'You can name yourself,' Llewellyn said. 'That's what we did!'

'If you were my toy soldier, I'd call you Morgan,' David suddenly said.

'Morgan,' Dilys repeated carefully. 'Yes – I like that. It's a good Welsh name, and you *are* a Welsh soldier after all. Even if you don't talk like one.'

'He's an officer – that's why he talks in

such a posh voice,' Llewellyn said, pointing to some faded painted stripes on Morgan's arm. 'Listen, Morgan, I hope this doesn't mean you're going to start ordering us all about,' he added, frowning.

'Wouldn't dream of it, old boy,' Morgan assured him hurriedly. 'Didn't even notice those stripes before, to tell you the truth. An officer, you say? Well, never mind that – all I want is for us all to be friends!'

'Look – the portal is starting to work again!' Myfanwy shrieked excitedly, and sure enough they could see now that the picnic ring was starting to glow very faintly.

'It really is working!' Ellie exclaimed, as the glow became stronger. 'We've done it!'

And to her amazement several of the fairies began to weep with relief as they realized they would be going home again after all.

When the museum room was finally empty
of fairies, Tedi told the children that the
toys would stay awake until the fairy dust
wore off, which depended how strong a
dose the fairies had given them in the first
place.

'While we're awake we've got something
to ask you,' Tedi said, suddenly looking
serious. 'You see, we're very worried about
Enid. Have you seen her since that old lady
took her away?'

Ellie told him about her visit to Mrs
Lloyd-Hughes's house. 'She seems to be

taking very good care of Enid,' she added, trying to reassure him.

'I'm sure Enid would much rather be back here with us, just the same,' Dilys said, frowning.

'We'll have to send the fairies to wake her up one night and ask her how she is,' Llewellyn suggested.

'We'd better not,' Tedi said. 'She might be upset if she wakes up and finds out that she's not in the museum any more.'

'Who *is* Enid?' Morgan wanted to know.

'She's a china doll who we used to tease a lot because she had ideas above her station,' Llewellyn told him, 'but she was one of us just the same – and we miss her terribly now she's gone.'

'Mr Owen said that the little girl who was Enid's first owner used to like pretending she was the Queen,' Ellie told them. 'That must be why Enid thought she was a royal doll.'

Just then Mr Daniels came into the room and the toys immediately stopped moving. 'Let's have a look at this soldier you've found then,' he said, coming over to peer into the cabinet. 'Where did you get him?'

'From Mr Owen,' Ellie explained. 'He's from the same regiment as the other one.'

'I can see that. Well, that's wonderful. I'll have to add him to my logbook!' He smiled at Ellie. 'I've just been on the phone to the local tourist office and they're going to help me advertise the museum. They say if I get some posters and flyers printed out then they'll distribute them for me. Maybe that way I'll get more visitors. I'm just off to tell my mother about it – she's been on at me for ages to advertise the museum a bit better

– and I wondered if you wanted to come with me. I know she'd be delighted to see you.' He looked uncertainly at David. 'And *you'd* be very welcome too, of course . . .'

'I think I'll just stay here, if that's all right,' David said quickly. 'I can look after the museum while you're gone, and I'll help design a poster if you like.'

'Well . . .' Mr Daniels looked unsure.

'David's really good at art,' Ellie pointed out. 'I bet he'll make you a fantastic poster!'

'Well, all right then,' Mr Daniels agreed. 'If you're sure you don't mind.'

David grinned and said that if he could borrow some paper and pencils then he would get started on the poster straight away.

At the nursing home they found Mrs Daniels in her bedroom, sitting in a large comfortable chair by the side of her bed. After Mr Daniels had chatted to her for a little while he said he was going off to do some errands in the village and would come back to collect Ellie in half an hour. That way Ellie and his mother could have their 'girlie' chat.

As soon as he had gone the old lady smiled at Ellie in a conspiratorial sort of a way. 'Well, my dear,' she began, 'I'm guessing you've met those fairies and seen their fairy portal in action by now, haven't you?'

Ellie nodded. 'I guessed you knew about them. Have you seen the toys coming alive too?'

'Oh, yes. I often went to the fairies' night-time parties when I was younger. It's just a pity my son doesn't believe in fairies. His father did, you know, but Daniel always thought the two of us were completely potty! Can you imagine a family where the parents believe in fairies, but the child doesn't? The fairies thought it was very funny, I can tell you!' She paused, suddenly looking more serious. 'But, Ellie, I'm very glad that you've come to see me again. I've been doing a bit of thinking since your last visit and I've decided there's something I want to give you.'

'*Give* me?'

'That's right. Remember I told you how our vicar found Dilys and Tedi when he was clearing out his loft?'

Ellie nodded.

'Well, there was something else that he found in that loft. It was a china doll that must also have been given to his wife for the church sale before she died. The vicar said I could have it for the museum, but it was so beautiful that I asked if I might

keep it for myself instead.'
She pointed at her
chest of drawers and
told Ellie to
open up the
bottom
one.

Ellie
opened
the
drawer
to find
a china
doll
wearing a bright
yellow dress – almost
identical to the one the fairies had made for
Enid. The doll had a sweet china face and
real blonde hair, with a parting that was
exactly in the middle, and when she lifted

up the dress Ellie found a pair of yellow knickers with the letter "H" embroidered on the front in pink thread.

Ellie looked up at Mrs Daniels, her cheeks flushed with excitement. 'It's "H" for Henrietta!' she exclaimed. 'The *real* Henrietta! *This* is Mrs Lloyd-Hughes's missing doll!'

Mr Daniels dropped Ellie off outside Mrs Lloyd-Hughes's house on the way back to the village and this time Mrs Lloyd-Hughes's housekeeper wasn't nearly so friendly when she opened the front door. 'I'm afraid she doesn't want to see you,' she told Ellie sharply.

'Well, will you please just show her this?' Ellie asked, handing over Henrietta.

'Another doll, eh? Well, stay here a moment then, and I'll see what she says.'

The housekeeper took the doll and disappeared inside the house, closing the door behind her.

As Ellie waited on the porch she strained her ears to try to hear what was happening inside – but she couldn't hear a thing.

A few minutes later the front door opened and the housekeeper appeared again, looking quite flustered. 'You've to come in,' she said, showing Ellie straight through to the living room.

To Ellie's relief, Mrs Lloyd-Hughes was sitting in her chair holding Henrietta up in front of her and smiling. In fact, the old lady seemed quite transformed, and as she turned to look at Ellie her eyes filled with tears. 'This is her!' she cried out, her voice husky with emotion. 'This is Henrietta!'

'I know,' Ellie said, feeling a little embarrassed by the old lady's outburst.

'There's even an "H" embroidered on her knickers.'

Mrs Lloyd-Hughes nodded. 'I did that myself when I was nine. I was only just learning to embroider. Wherever did you find her?'

So Ellie told her how Mrs Daniels had been given Henrietta by the vicar when he was moving out of the vicarage fifty years earlier. 'Your mother must have given her to the vicar's wife for the church sale – and then *she* died so the sale never happened. So Henrietta was

put up in the loft along with all the other things, and forgotten about for the next twenty years, until the vicar gave her to Mrs Daniels – who didn't know she belonged to you, of course.'

'Poor Henrietta,' Mrs Lloyd-Hughes said. 'I still can't believe you've found her!'

'Mrs Daniels wanted *me* to have her,' Ellie said. 'But she says you can keep her if you like – so long as you give me Enid in exchange for her.'

'Enid?'

'The *other* china doll.'

'Of course, of course!' the old lady readily agreed.

So Ellie picked up Enid and said goodbye to Mrs Lloyd-Hughes. And as she left it seemed to Ellie that the old lady was hugging Henrietta as if she was a long-lost child rather than just a doll.

13

That night as Ellie and David lay in bed talking they both agreed that their holiday in Wales had been far more exciting than they could ever have thought possible.

By the time Ellie had got back to the museum with Enid that morning, David had sketched a very good picture of them for Mr Daniels to put on his posters. Mr Daniels had offered to let Ellie keep Enid for herself, but Ellie had turned down his offer, saying that Enid belonged in the museum. She had asked Mr Daniels to put Enid back in the cabinet, smiling to herself as she thought of the lovely surprise the toys were going to get the next time they woke up and found her there.

'You see, Enid might not be able to come to life if she came back home to live with me,' Ellie told her brother now. 'I mean, *I've* never seen any fairies at home – have you?'

'No,' David agreed. 'Though I must say, I've never actually looked.'

As he spoke they saw a movement at the window, and Bronwen and Myfanwy suddenly flew into the room.

'Queen Lily is throwing a massive fairy party in the toy museum tonight to celebrate the fact that we don't have to leave this valley after all!' Myfanwy told them excitedly. 'And she wants you to come!'

'Yes – and there's something at the party that she really wants you to see!' Bronwen added, beaming at Ellie.

'What is it?' Ellie asked, throwing back her duvet.

'It's a secret until you get there,' Myfanwy replied, giggling.

Suddenly Ellie heard a familiar neighing coming from outside. 'Is the flying pony here again?' she asked, rushing to the window where she looked out and saw the same pony as before. Only this time he was harnessed up to a beautiful golden carriage, and instead of wheels the carriage had a pair of wings that was flapping along with the pony's.

'Queen Lily said he was too small to carry both of you, so she's sent a magic carriage as well,' Bronwen explained.

David had come to the window too now, and since he had never seen a flying pony before – let alone a flying carriage – he was so shocked he couldn't even speak.

'Hurry up – everyone's waiting for you,' Myfanwy told them, whizzing across to the dressing table and picking up David's camera.

'Careful with that,' David said. 'And you'll have to wait while we get dressed first. I'm not going to a party in my pyjamas!'

'Oh, don't worry about that! The fairy dressmakers have made you both party outfits. You can change when we get there,' Bronwen said.

'What *sort* of party outfits?' David asked, sounding dubious, but since Ellie had already climbed into the carriage, he

decided he had better join her before it flew off and left him behind.

When they arrived at the museum Bronwen and Myfanwy ushered them into the office, where they found two party outfits that were just the right size for them, hanging on two sparkly coat hangers.

David's outfit consisted of a gold-coloured waistcoat, a frilly blue shirt and dark blue silky trousers, and when he saw it he pulled a face. 'I might have known it would be really uncool.'

'Shh!' Ellie whispered. 'The fairies might hear you!' Her own outfit was a beautiful yellow party dress – with matching yellow shoes – and when she touched the material she could tell that it was made from daffodil petals just like the fairies' own dresses. Somehow they must have sewn lots of petals together, though the seams were quite invisible, and when Ellie slipped the dress over her head she could even smell the scent of daffodils. 'I love this dress!' she exclaimed. And she wished there was a mirror in Mr Daniels's office so that she could see herself in it. 'I wonder if the dress would show up in a photograph,' she said, picking up David's camera, which he had taken from Myfanwy while they were in the carriage.

'Well, I definitely don't want a photo-graph of me dressed like this,' David grumbled to himself as he put on the shirt, trousers and waistcoat. 'Leave the camera here, Ellie.'

When they were both ready, they opened the door to find Myfanwy and Bronwen waiting for them outside.

'You both look lovely!' Bronwen exclaimed.

'Especially you, David!' Myfanwy gushed. 'Now you can dance with me! Come on! The party's this way!'

The doors swung open and the children saw that the room had been completely transformed. Fairy lights were strung across the ceiling and walls, and sparkly bunting decorated the tops of all the cabinets. Musical notes made from fairy dust kept appearing and then disappearing like flashing lights, as beautiful dance music filled the room. Ellie's toy friends were out of their cabinet and dancing along with the fairies. Ellie spotted Enid (who was back in her own blue dress again) and Dilys, both wearing glittery party hats as they danced a jig with Tedi, whose hat kept slipping down over his eyes so that he was bumping into everybody. Llewellyn and Morgan both looked very smart in their shiny painted uniforms as they tried to teach their fairy dance partners to do their favourite dance – the military two-step.

A large picnic rug had been spread out at the far end of the room and the dolls' tea set from the other night was there, along with several fairy-sized cups. In the centre of the rug was a very fancy cake that had to be at least ten layers tall. Each layer seemed to be hovering in place by itself and on the very top of the cake was a life-size sugar daffodil.

Queen Lily was sitting on a large sparkly cushion at one end of the picnic rug and when she saw the children she clapped her hands and the fairy music stopped abruptly.

'Before we continue with our party, I want to say a big thank-you to Ellie – on behalf of all of us – for saving our museum!' she announced, flying up into the air and spreading out her wings as she beamed at the children.

'And thank-you for bringing Enid back to us!' Tedi called out, as Enid waved and smiled at her gratefully.

'Yes!' Myfanwy shouted. 'Now that we have Enid *and* Morgan, our fairy portal is even safer!'

'HIP-HIP-HURRAH FOR ELLIE!' all the fairies shouted at once. And then came the deafening noise of all of them clapping.

'You wouldn't think fairies could *make* such a noise, would you?' David whispered, and Ellie giggled in agreement.

'SPEECH! SPEECH!' the fairies were all shouting, and it was clear they expected Ellie to say something.

'Do you want me to do it for you?' David asked, knowing how shy his sister was about speaking in public.

'No, it's OK,' Ellie replied, because suddenly she realized something. She realized that although she *did* feel shy – so shy that she could feel herself blushing furiously – she also *really* wanted to tell the fairies herself how glad she was to have been able to help them.

So she did.

After Ellie had finished speaking, David whispered, 'Well done!' in her ear.

'That's it, Ellie!' the fairy queen said,

smiling at her. '*That's* the thing I wanted you to come to the party to see!'

'How do you mean?' Ellie asked, not understanding.

'You have conquered your shyness,' Queen Lily told her. 'Otherwise, how could you have made such a lovely speech?'

And as Ellie realized this was true, all the fairies started to cheer and clap again.

'Come and dance with me, David!' Myfanwy called out to him as the music started up. She flew across to sprinkle dancing dust over his feet, and he soon found himself dancing more energetically – and more uncoolly – than he had ever danced before.

'Where are you going, Ellie?' he called out as he spotted his sister hurrying towards the door.

'To fetch your camera!' Ellie called back

laughing, because there was no way she was missing out on getting a photograph of *this*.

Turn the page to read...
some of Gwyneth Rees's secret stuff

☆ ☆

Five things you didn't know about Gwyneth...

1. Gwyneth has been writing children's books since she was ten years old.
2. Her favourite ice-cream flavour is Toffee Deluxe.
3. She has two cats called Magnus and Hattie.
4. When she was born, she was nearly called Myfanwy instead of Gwyneth.
5. She used to be able to do the Highland Fling (but now she's forgotten most of the steps)!

Gwyneth's five favourite children's books are ...

1. *The Secret Garden* by Frances Hodgson Burnett
2. *The Silver Sword* by Ian Serraillier
3. *Journey to the River Sea* by Eva Ibbotson
4. *Goggle-eyes* by Anne Fine
5. *Little Women* by Louisa M. Alcott

Gwyneth's five top tips for writing are...

1. Make some kind of plan before you start – it usually helps!
2. Write about something you're interested in.
3. Make your readers care about the main character.
4. Don't be afraid to go back and make changes after you've written your story – or while you're still writing it!
5. Try reading it out loud yourself to see how it sounds. Then try reading it out loud to someone you trust. If they laugh in the right places and don't drift off, then that's a good story!

Gwyneth's five favourite facts...

1. Fairies absolutely love chocolate – just like Gwyneth does!
2. Fairies start out as little bundles of joy who get looked after by fairy nannies in fairy nurseries.
3. You have to believe in fairies to see them – and that makes it extra magical when you do!
4. Children have to be shrunk down to the size of a fairy with fairy dust in order to visit Fairyland.
5. Dream fairies have the best shoes, which they make magically using shoe dust.

And finally, Gwyneth's great big, silly secret that she'd never want anyone to know about her EVER

(but we're going to tell you anyway)

is ...

when she was little she nearly set the kitchen on fire by trying to dry her wet shoes under the grill! Oops!

Gwyneth Rees
fairy treasure

Connie has never believed in fairies, so she is amazed when Ruby, a tiny fairy-girl, suddenly appears in the library of the old house where Connie is staying.

Ruby says that she is a book fairy – but that she is in terrible trouble. She has been banished from fairyland until she finds a ruby ring which she has lost.

Can Connie help Ruby find the missing ring – before the doorway to fairyland is closed forever?

Gwyneth Rees

fairy dreams

Evie had always believed in fairies,
but she has never seen one . . .

When Grandma is taken into hospital, Evie finds herself sleeping in Grandma's old brass bed – and being visited by Moonbeam and Star, two dream fairies who whisk her away on a magical journey to Queen Celeste's palace in fairyland.

Moonbeam and Star tell Evie they can't make Grandma better, but they can give her a wonderful adventure so long as she is sleeping in a magic bed. Can Evie find a way to make Grandma's fairy dreams come true?

A selected list of titles available from Macmillan Children's Books

The prices shown below are correct at the time of going to press. However, Macmillan Publishers reserves the right to show new retail prices on covers, which may differ from those previously advertised.

Gwyneth Rees

Fairy Dust	978-0-330-41554-5	£4.99
Fairy Treasure	978-0-330-43730-1	£4.99
Fairy Dreams	978-0-330-43476-8	£4.99
Fairy Gold	978-0-330-43938-0	£4.99
Fairy Rescue	978-0-330-43971-8	£4.99
Mermaid Magic (3 books in 1)	978-0-330-42632-9	£4.99
Cosmo and the Magic Sneeze	978-0-330-43729-5	£4.99
Cosmo and the Great Witch Escape	978-0-330-43733-2	£4.99
The Magical Book of Fairy Fun	978-0-330-44421-7	£4.99
Cosmo's Book of Spooky Fun	978-0-330-45123-9	£4.99

For older readers

The Mum Hunt	978-0-330-41012-0	£4.99
The Mum Detective	978-0-330-43453-9	£4.99
The Mum Mystery	978-0-330-44212-1	£4.99
My Mum's from Planet Pluto	978-0-330-43728-8	£4.99
The Making of May	978-0-330-43732-5	£4/00

All Pan Macmillan titles can be ordered from our website, www.panmacmillan.com, or from your local bookshop and are also available by post from:

Bookpost, PO Box 29, Douglas, Isle of Man IM99 1BQ

Credit cards accepted. For details:
Telephone: 01624 677237
Fax: 01624 670923
Email: bookshop@enterprise.net
www.bookpost.co.uk

Free postage and packing in the United Kingdom